Two Birds With One Stone

by

Sigrid Vansandt

Dedication

To my most wonderful cousin, Stacey, and my dear friend, Sheila. Without your generous hearts, talents, and fierce determination, I would never have been able to write, edit, format, upload and manage this book. You are my best critics, cheerleaders, mentors, and friends. Thank you from the bottom of my heart for leading the way, taking my hand and guiding me, and giving me something only truly generous hearts can give: hope and love.

Sig

Cover Design by Jenny McGee
Copyright © cover images 2019 by Jenny McGee
See more of Jenny's work at **artistjennymcgee.com**

Table of Contents

Chapter 1

Hayworth, England
March 5, 1855

Married less than a year and pregnant, Charlotte was
wasting away. At only thirty-eight, her health was dwindling
fast. Weak from the incessant vomiting and coughing of blood, it
was with a great effort, she lifted herself from the bed and went to
her bureau to search for Emily's manuscript.

Finding it under the chemises, she gently wrapped it and
lovingly tucked it into a shallow leather box. The last time the
manuscript had seen the light of day was during Charlotte and
Arthur's first days back at home after their honeymoon. Arthur,
her husband, wished to read it. He'd always been critical of
Emily's work and after reading a short section, he said it should
be burned. Charlotte refused to let him, but now that she was so
weak, he might take matters into his own hands while she was
incapable of stopping him. Something deep in her mind, in a
corner she wasn't comfortable visiting, made her want to protect
the book from even her own husband.

The publishers Emily contacted before her death were still
pressing Charlotte about the manuscript. They were eager to have
a sequel to *Wuthering Heights*, but she was uncertain whether to
proceed or not. Society wasn't comfortable with a woman writing,
thinking, and feeling the way Emily had done. It was curious to
Charlotte, as she considered her sister's lovely handwriting on the
opening page, how Emily's work either ignited a passionate desire
to love it or an equally passionate desire to destroy it.

For the time being, it would need a safe place to rest until
Charlotte could decide what to do. The best place to keep it safe
would be the secret spot in the wainscot that she and her siblings

used to hide things from their father many long years ago when they were only children.

Her hands trembled as she cradled the leather box. Dear, lost faces rose up in Charlotte's mind as the box whispered with familiar voices from the past. Maybe her memory yoked with the solidity of the box would work an enchantment, allowing her to break the bitter spell of her sibling's deaths. Her mind flooded with longing for the times she'd spent with her sisters and brother. She owed Emily the book's safety.

Quietly she tiptoed across the room, careful to avoid the creaky spots in the floor. Everyone downstairs would be wondering what she was up to, if they heard her moving about too much. Charlotte should be resting and Aurthur would become curious, too curious.

She had debated with herself so many times since Emily's death what to do with the last manuscript her sister finished, and once their baby was born and her health returned, Charlotte must make the final decision.

To the left of the fender disguised as a knothole was the latch. A soft smile brushed her face as she remembered how much fun it had been to hide something from the adults when she was a girl.

All one had to do was pull out the wooden knot in the panel with something sharp like a letter opener, insert your pinky into the hole and pull. As she opened the small door, the smells of musty, long-forgotten papers mingled together. Like a shy child, the scent timidly greeted her nose as the tomb of her childhood opened up once more. There, shoved within, was an old-fashioned magazine still hidden from her father's eyes. A forgotten thing of childhood fancies.

"Charlotte! Are you in bed?" came a concerned man's voice from the landing.

His call sent a shock wave through her wearied brain. Anxiety twisted the cord of tension between her mind and stomach, creating a burst of energy. She focused to complete her task.

6

Her hands and brain moved efficiently. Pushing the old papers to the back, she made a fragile nest for the box and closed the door studying it intently to make sure it wouldn't give up its secrets due to a misalignment or a tear in the varnish. She prayed the existence of the hiding place was unknown to anyone other than her now that her siblings were gone.

Exhausted from her exertions, Charlotte crossed the bedroom and lay herself back down on the bed. With one last furtive glance at the secret place in the wainscot, she shut her eyes and prayed that, like King Minos, she'd hidden her truth where only a hero might dare to enter. The last thought that crossed her mind before she slept was to remember to write Ellen, her dearest friend. Ellen should know about everything. Soon Charlotte was drifted off to aslccp.

A soft click of the door latch revealed a face peering in on Charlotte's sleeping figure. Authur scanned the bedchamber. His expression was pensive as he scrutinized the room's interior. Finding nothing amiss, he pulled back and shut the door. For a while longer, beauty and truth would sleep hidden in a dusty hole safe from the ignorance, insecurity and greed of human agencies.

Chapter 2

Marsden-Lacey, Yorkshire, England
Present Day

Martha Littleword tucked the newspaper she bought at the news agent's under her arm. She strutted down the High Street of Marsden-Lacey with an air of victory. Her red hair tried its best to escape the lopsided bun wobbling on top of her head.

"That little mongrel never saw it coming," she thought to herself triumphantly.

The image of her attacker rolling and groaning in the street next to the news agent's stand made her chuckle deliciously under her breath. Those self-defense classes at the Village Community Centre actually worked. She was surprised with herself as she was sure the young tough who attacked her must have been when he lunged for her purse and she neatly laid him out cold in the gutter.

Ralph, the news agent, had recognized the teenager as Sam Berry, a local hooligan. Ralph couldn't get over what Martha managed to do. He just stood there looking back and forth between Martha and the sprawled-out miscreant, Sam, repeating mostly to himself, "You," and then looking at the teenage boy unconscious in the street, "He." Then more as if questioning the truth of what he saw, "You?" and then "Sam?"

Martha with her usual pragmatism finally answered, "Yeah, Ralph, me."

Dishing back the attacker's assault had been remarkably easy. Martha had been standing talking to Ralph Emerson, a harmless but long-winded town gossip who was dropping innuendos about the new curator at The Grange, when a tremendous push from behind propelled Martha toward a surprised and open-mouthed Ralph. Then a firm jerk on her arm pulled her back toward her center of gravity and with a turn of her body, she did an about-face.

Acting out of instinct, she pulled hard on the purse, forcing her attacker off-balance. Like a huge fish caught on a line, the boy came reeling toward Martha's five foot frame. She brought up her knee and neatly dealt a crushing blow to his manhood and finished him off with an interlocking fist blow to the top of his rather mangy head.

It was an amazing feat of athleticism and it was over in less than thirty-seconds. As a crowd gathered around with wide-eyed stares and the usual comments, she found herself a bit unsure of what she'd actually done. Only when Ralph started his monosyllabic utterances did Martha snap back to herself like a rubber band and retrieved her purse. A sense of delight and weightlessness followed infusing her whole self with joy at what she'd done.

The police arrived. A young constable she recognized from her self-defense classes asked questions. After she gave her short statement to the police, she left the pitiful, human heap known as Sam for the police constable and Ralph to deal with, and continued with her original intentions up the High Street toward The Grange where she had an appointment with its new curator.

Martha's reflections on the experience began to take on a mythological aura which was partly due to her natural proclivity to enhance a story until it met with her standards of drama and with her propensity, like most humans, to enjoy a rare moment of self-pride. But her ego, happily for Martha, was fraught with attention deficit issues, so as she climbed the street, her steps became less reflective of a victory march and more in line with her usual upright and eager self.

Her dress was professional and her shoes were the necessary black, low-heeled things required by the law office she worked in as a paralegal. Walking felt good. It stretched out the catch in her back. Lately, she'd begun to recognize subtle physical changes and life was a bit stale since her daughter was away at school. Taking the thug down in the High Street was a nice way of

9

rebalancing the cosmic bottom line in her favor and gave her eyes a nice twinkle of life to them. Naturally, Martha was in fine spirits as she finally ascended the High Street hill and entered the iron gates of The Grange, Marsden-Lacey's newest and, for that matter, only museum.

She walked in through the entrance of the lovely, old Elizabethan manor home which had recently been turned into a repository for rare nineteenth-century manuscripts and books. A rush of cool air immediately enveloped her and she hesitated in the hall to allow her eyes to adjust. Slowly, the beautiful oak paneling and the worn flagstones came into view. She wondered, for what must have been the millionth time, at how divine these old manor houses were in England.

In the corner of the hall was an elegant but newly constructed reception desk built in a semicircle and made to conform to the rest of the hall's architecture. She rang the bell on the desk and peeked over the edge. No one was around. Since the receptionist must be out, Martha decided to snoop about a bit. She walked down the main hallway toward two sizable and ornately decorated mahogany doors, and with a quick look around to see if anyone might be watching her, she laid her ear against the door and listened.

Martha could make out a woman's voice on the other side. She gently opened the door to peer inside. There stood a slim brunette with her back to Martha. Her cell phone was pressed to her ear. The woman was American. It was always nice to hear the old, familiar accent, and from the sound of it, the woman was probably from somewhere a hair south of the Mason-Dixon Line.

Years of working in the law field had given Martha ample experience in reading people. At first she thought the woman was an uptight, academic type. Shoes without any scuffs, neatly pressed spot-free blouse, and a perfectly coiffed hairstyle, certainly gave the woman the appearance of someone who practiced an acute attention to detail. But in an instant Martha saw there was something finer under the professional layers. From the woman's body language and the tone of her voice, she must be talking to someone very familiar to her, probably a family member or possibly a child.

The slim brunette slumped slightly as if she was tired and worn down from life's daily trials which unwittingly engendering a sense of empathy in Martha for her. Moving softly away from the door, but not so far as to miss too much of the conversation, Martha patiently waited. The hallway was cool and pleasant. Nothing moved for a minute or two then a wasp buzzed near her ear and she swatted at it.

"Go back outside," she said firmly to the insect. "You're trouble and I've already taken one of your kind down today. Don't tempt me for a second time."

The woman was finished with her call, Martha pulled back the door and went inside while the wasp took flight in search for weaker things to prey upon.

Chapter 3

Hayworth, England
March 31, 1855

Ellen Nussey, Charlotte's dearest friend through life, had received the letter from Charlotte's father, Reverend Brontë, informing her Charlotte was dying. He made it sound as if she would be gone within the day.

Ellen wanted to be there when Charlotte died. They'd loved each other as sisters and shared all their secrets since their school days. Ellen knew deep in her soul the importance of getting to Hayworth before Charlotte passed. If she didn't make it, so much would be lost.

Arthur Bell Nicholls, Charlotte's husband, had increasingly censored his wife's correspondence for the last few months of their marriage. He castigated Charlotte for the openness of the subject matter in her letters to Ellen. In the end, he requested of Ellen that every letter she receive be immediately burned after reading.

Ellen had promised to obey his request because she realized he was the worst kind of man: a bully and a zealot who would never recognize the greatness of his wife's gift or worse, he was jealous of it. The only way to deal with a tyrant like Reverend Nicholls was to let him think she was compliant. Otherwise, he would restrict Charlotte's only means of expression and communication.

When Ellen arrived at the parsonage, Charlotte had already passed. Her grief for her friend was absolute. Nicholls was in truth devastated by his wife's death. He still clung to her tiny, wasted hand. Charlotte lay quiet and peaceful, free finally from the horrific and grueling suffering she'd endured for her last months of life.

As Ellen stood above her dear, brilliant friend, a terrific shock of realization came to her. It was only a matter of time before Nicholls would comb through Charlotte's letters, papers, and memorabilia, and burn them all. From Ellen's vantage point, looking down upon the grieving husband's head, the truth of what she must do to save Charlotte's work stormed through her mind. Feigning the need to lie down due to grief, she asked if she might go up to the old nursery. Charlotte's father offered to show her up but she declined saying she well-remembered the way.

Once in the old room, a hundred happy memories came to her but she didn't have time for any of that now. She shooed them away and went straight for the hidden place in the wainscot. Charlotte alluded to this place in one of her last letters to Ellen. At the time Ellen thought the letter was odd, but after some rereading, Ellen realized Charlotte couldn't be forthright in her correspondence anymore and was trying to tell Ellen something.

It took some time to locate the small hole in the wall but she found it and, placing her finger into the hole, she opened the hidden panel. There, wrapped and boxed, was the thing Charlotte deemed so important she couldn't dare name it in her letter.

Ellen lifted it out and opened the lid. There wrapped in one of Charlotte's own chemises was Emily's last manuscript. Sheer fear gripped Ellen's mind. She couldn't openly carry it out of the house. How could she transport it? An idea sprung into her mind. Lifting her skirt, she tore long strands from her cotton petticoats and tied the box securely to the inside of her upper thigh. It was awkward, but once all her undergarments were in place, it was impossible to tell she had anything hidden on her person.

Later that day, Ellen Nussey gave her condolences to the father and husband of her most-beloved friend. She departed the Hayworth Parsonage and never looked back. She tried to find it in her heart to forgive Charlotte's husband for his stupidity and inflated sense of self. It didn't matter, because even Charlotte had realized the limitations of her husband and had acted responsibly in the end. She'd gotten through to the one person she knew she could trust: her friend.

Ellen wouldn't let her down. She would keep the manuscript and all of Charlotte's letters safe. As the chase she was driving fought its way over the hard, dirt road, Ellen meticulously planned how she would secure the items from Authur's inquests regarding their whereabouts. Fortunately, she was successful and her efforts saved for the world some of the most treasured works of art it has ever known.

Chapter 4

Marsden-Lacey, England
Present Day

Helen Ryes pursed her lips and raised her eyebrows as she read the incoming number on her mobile. She'd just finished a call from her daughter and now Timothy, her youngest, who lived in Concord, Massachusetts, way trying to reach her. With a deeply-resigned, maternal sigh, she brushed the glass surface of her device and asked, "Yes, Timothy?"

"Mother. Why aren't you answering your phone for God's sake?"

"I just got off the phone with Christine and I'm working. You do remember your mother works, dear?"

"Oh, my God, of course I know you work, but you've been avoiding all of our phone calls because you don't want to attend Dad's wedding."

As the diatribe continued from her loving child, Helen held the phone slightly away from her ear and examined the back of her hand. She thought about how nice it would be to have a manicure and then, why not a pedicure, too? Something to give order to her life at the moment would be so nice.

Once she realized the barking and whining had slowed on the other end of the line, she returned the phone to her ear, careful to avoid her pearl earring.

"Darling, Mama's not going to Daddy's beach-side shindig." Her temper stoked itself on visions of the happy couple's matrimonial bliss being paid for by her hard work. The thought of her ex-husband, George, standing probably in sandals and a flowery shirt made her want to force feed him every bill he'd left for her to pay when he ran off with her assistant Fiona.

Trying to be loving but firm, Helen's words took on the impression of an irritated, albeit a loving mother, who was tired of her cub's meddling with things he would be better off leaving alone.

"You see, dear, I'm not paying to travel to some God-forsaken Floridian swamp to wish Fiona and your father happy trails. Not at my expense anyway, and why Florida? Why does everyone want to go to Florida? It's hot and everyone ends up burned. In this case quite literally."

"You know it's not about the wedding, Mother."

"Oh, dear, what exactly is it about then?" Helen tersely asked.

"Seeing your grandchild, maybe. Seeing your children possibly. I don't know, Mother. Maybe seeing *your* family."

This last fuming howl touched Helen and cooled her temper. Timothy's sweet, six-year-old, dirt-encrusted face swam up from her memory. She saw him again as he was the day she found him sitting in the garden digging for worms. Remembering how she had pulled Timothy into her arms, the feel of his small neck against her cheek and the soft smell of sunshine, fresh air and little boy mingling together made an elixir for maternal love. The memory hung there for a moment and Helen's tone shifted.

She said gently, "Darling, I'll need some time. You do understand? Don't you, Timothy? I need some time. Of course I want more than anything to see all of you. I'll let you know. Give me a few days. Fiona and George," she said these last two names with a definite hint of irritation, "aren't marrying for another two weeks. I've got time to think it through still."

"All right, Mom. We want to see you and I know Christine and Peter are planning to be there. It wouldn't be the same without you." This last part faded away to a small crack in his voice.

Helen knew her children were suffering, too. Their parent's divorce and George's quick decision to marry his new-found love, a woman half his age, had come out of the blue. George was trying to grab back his youth or maybe he'd been miserable in his

16

marriage with Helen. Either way, the last year had been tough on the entire family and everyone was having to wrestle with new ways of living.

In a soothing maternal voice, Helen said, "I'll let you know, dear. Don't worry. It'll all be fine. I love you, Timmy. Let's talk later and I promise to see you all one way or the other." With a forced attempt to finish with a bright last note she touched "end" on the phone.

"Hmph." Someone cleared her throat. Helen spun around to see a conventionally-dressed, curvy but short woman in her forties. Red hair was piled on the top of her head slightly askew with springing whispies flying out in every direction. It was as if she had been in a wind storm or had been wrestling with something, Helen thought to herself.

"Hello. I'm sorry to interrupt, but there isn't a receptionist at the desk. My name is Martha Littleword. I'm with Partridge, Sims & Cuthbirt. I'm trying to locate Mr. Louis Devry, the curator?" This last bit was said with an apologetic, upward rise in her tone.

"Oh, yes, of course, I'm Helen Ryes. I'm the book conservator," Helen returned. "He just stepped out saying he wouldn't be back for the day. He seemed a bit preoccupied. Is there anything I might help you with?"

"Well first, I'd like to say it's always nice to run into a fellow American," Martha said with a warm smile.

"How nice. What part of the States are you from?" Helen asked returning the smile with an outstretched hand which Martha took giving it a firm shake.

It was like finding an old friend in the last place you expected.

"Everyone calls me Martha, by the way. I'm from Arkansas, the northwest corner, a small town called Grace. What about you?"

"No! Me too. Ever heard of Evening Shade?" Helen asked her smile now brighter than before.

17

"On the other side of Conway? I do know it. Small world," Martha said giving her head a shake. "So, do you work here at The Grange?"

"Not exactly. I'm a private contractor. I assess and provide conservation work on books or in this case, entire libraries. The Grange has one of the best libraries in England representing nineteenth-century authors. I was thrilled to be offered the chance to sniff around the place and work on this collection. One never knows what might turn up in these old collections."

Helen showed Martha two of the books she was currently preparing for conservation. One was a first-edition poetry book by Percy Bysshe Shelley titled "Queen Mab." The other was a diary of a navy admiral stationed in Singapore during Britain's heyday of imperialism.

"I've probably been boring you. I'll talk your leg off, if you're not careful." Helen laid the diary down on a piece of pristine cotton fabric. "Should we go find the receptionist, Mary, and see what Mr. Devry's calendar looks like?"

"I'm supposed to take Mr. Devry's statement in a case I'm working on," Martha explained as they walked back down the hall. "I guess I missed him because of a 'to-do' that happened on the way here. It slowed me down."

Helen's eyebrows furrowed as she recalled her last conversation with Mr. Devry. He hadn't mentioned any legal issues but then why would he? Devry had, if anything, been extremely reserved and aloof, not exactly the talkative type the entire week she'd worked at The Grange.

"So Mary wasn't at her desk when you came in?" Helen asked.

"No one was about."

"She's probably returned. Her lunch hour is usually around one o'clock or two."

At the end of the corridor, the somber coolness of The Grange's entrance hall was offset by the warm sunlight and summer breeze floating in through the open door to the main entrance. Sounds of bees working diligently at their pollen duties

18

on the hollyhocks near the entrance mixed with the everyday noises wafting up from the village below. The women's eyes had to adjust as they came into the hall. Light from the outside made the dark walls and stone floor recede into shadows.

Together their gazes fell upon a multiple array of water droplets splattered on the floor and leading behind the semicircular reception desk. As they got closer, the water appeared to be discolored. Some instinct made Helen stoop down and touch one. Bringing her hand up to her still light-dazzled eyes, she saw the red stain on her fingers.

"Oh, my God." Helen said, her voice raw and staccato. "It's blood."

"What?" Martha asked in a breathless whisper.

Helen raised her hand to show to reveal the smeared blood on her fingers.

The two women's gazes locked in mutual horror and it was Martha who first moved behind the reception desk. There, lying on the ground, was a well-dressed man face down in a pool of blood.

Martha looked up at Helen and said throatily, "Call the police."

Dialing the emergency number with trembling fingers, Helen put her phone up against her ear. A man answered and Helen blurted out, "There's a man dead. There's so much blood. Here, at The Grange and…and…he's been murdered."

Chapter 5

Detective Chief Inspector Merriam Johns had been on the force for almost twenty-five years. He never enjoyed dealing with distressed women and he especially disliked distressed foreign women who had gone and involved themselves in local crimes. As he saw it, they should keep their noses clean when visiting foreign places and his village in particular.

The more he imagined what the woman on the other end of the phone must be like, the more his colicky self escalated into a temper. She was definitely an American and that always meant an extra hassle. Americans were usually one of two things: half were curious about every minute aspect of the British police investigation experience as if it were a TV drama and all cops in England were Sherlock Holmes; the other half loved to comment on how American cops did things differently. He wished he had a pound for every time some American had said, "Well, we don't do it that way in America."

These kind of thoughts increased his irritation level making his temper rise. He remembered his doctor's advice about getting worked up and his blood pressure.

"Not good for the old ticker," Doc Whithersby said while pointing toward his own heart or where there should have been one.

He wondered if Whithersby was serious about his, Johns', ticker or if he was insidious enough to make Johns question his own health. He and Whithersby had been in a tight competition for Lilly Peterson, the bartender at The Traveller's Inn.

The thoughts of Lilly began to sooth his cantankerous soul as Johns turned his vehicle up the High Street. He pulled up in front of The Grange, turned off the siren and got out of the car. The ambulance was right behind him.

Due to an injury caused by chasing one of the village teens through Mr. and Mrs. Down's garden (local nudists) last summer, Johns walked with a slight stiffness in his right leg. This along with his extremely stout, bulldog, six-foot tall body, he gave the impression of a slow, determined, military tank forcefully moving through the lower parking area.

Thinking about Lilly, he ran his bear paw of a hand through his buzz-cut hair. Not more than an inch long on any point of his scalp, each black hair stood perfectly at attention. It was nice to be able to count on something and Johns' hair was a definite constant in his life.

He headed for the upper level of the old Grange's gardens and prepared himself for what lay ahead by putting on an expression of grumpy boredom. Somehow that always relaxed people and made them think he had the problem well in hand. The woman had said it was murder. Johns shook his head from side to side. What were things coming to these days? First, some woman body-slammed some mugger in the village market place and now murder at one of Marsden-Lacey's most famous landmarks?

A wasp landed on Johns' forearm. Without a second thought, he flicked it to the ground and stepped on it not even breaking his stride as he continued his march up to The Grange's front entrance.

Scene break

Martha and Helen had sat quietly on the bench after calling the police. They focused intently on the modern digital clock hanging over the reception area. The body behind the desk gave a sickening feeling to the room. It was impossible to not be constantly aware of the dead man behind the desk.

Soon distant sirens could be heard. They both shifted uneasily in their places, unsure of what to expect when the police arrived.

Martha, light-headed, laid her head against the oak paneled wall. She looked over at Helen who was also resting her head

21

against the cool paneling, her jaw slightly slack. Out of nowhere, Martha felt an uncontrollable urge to laugh. Unnerved by her reaction, she fought to control it, but a snort and a chuckle slipped out anyway. It brought Helen out of her stupor with a start and she turned to look at Martha with wide, incredulous eyes.

"Did you just laugh?" she asked in a shocked tone.

Martha quickly put her hand over her offending mouth and mumbled through it. "Oh, God. I'm sorry. I looked at your face and I don't know. It hit me as funny. I'm sorry. It's not funny. I know that. Okay, I don't know why I'm laughing. This is horrible."

"You're hysterical," Helen blurted out bluntly and again rested her head against the paneling.

In unintentional unison, they both sucked in deep breaths and exhaled. Immediately, they both burst out laughing. The laughter, albeit bad timing, decompressed their tension for a short time until blaring sirens, tires crunching on the gravel outside, and voices calling to each other announced the arrival of the emergency team and the police.

Martha's nose twitched. An overbearing smell of aftershave wafted into the room.

"Whoa. Someone practically bathed in the stuff," she said. As if on cue, the breeze delivered the concentrated form of Detective Chief Inspector Johns through the front door.

"Where is it?" Johns asked in a commanding tone.

Both Helen and Martha jumped up from their seats and began to walk toward him.

"Behind the desk," Helen said and pointing with a trembling finger.

The room became busy with the police and emergency task force.

Johns knelt down to check the man's pulse. "Either of you check to see if he was dead during the last ten minutes?"

Martha and Helen exchanged nervous, shocked looks, both immediately realizing they had never checked for a pulse.

"Get a stretcher in here," Johns said to the sergeant standing near the door. "This murdered man isn't quite dead...yet."

Chapter 6

London, England
1898

Peter Dutton, solicitor for Laughton, Audley & Dutton, opened the letter from Thomas Gunn, an estate agent located in West Yorkshire. He read as follows:

23 January 1898
Moor Lane House, England

Laughton, Audley & Dutton
Solicitors, Middle Temple Lane, London.

Honored Sirs:

I take this opportunity to inform you of our completion in cataloguing the estate of Miss Ellen Nussey. We have employed the respectable estate agents of Howard & Sons to prepare the premises for auction. Weather permitting, the first of March should give sufficient time to advertise the event properly.

Along with many nice household items, Miss Nussey has a substantial collection of correspondence and written materials from her friendship with Charlotte Brontë and the Brontë family. It may be wise to handle these items separately by employing a London agent to find a proper buyer.

Enclosed you will find a detailed account of each item as you requested and I take the liberty of sending you the Brontë curios by way of my assistant, Mr. Wallins. We await your approval of our endeavors and any further requests.

Respectfully,
Mr. Thomas Gunn, Solicitor,
Brathwait & Co Solicitors

As Dutton lay the letter on his desk, he considered the package Gunn's assistant delivered that morning. Gunn managed to clear up the estate quite well and recognized the importance of the Brontë items correctly.

Dutton called in his clerk. "Perkins, take these items to Hodgson & Company, the book auctioneers. Tell them to find an appropriate buyer."

The clerk took the packages and did as he was told. Both items were sold later that year to Amy Lowell, a poet and socialite living in Brookline, Massachusetts.

Chapter 7

Marsden-Lacey, England
Present Day

"Alive? He's alive? Oh my God! We left him there for dead," Helen said, taking a turn at sounding a bit hysterical.

Johns eyed the two women critically. Littleword was pretty, although kind of buxom for his taste, and the brunette seemed uptight. They were both around forty, and didn't look like fledgling murderers but until he had more information, he wouldn't rule them out.

With a glint in his eyes, Johns pointed to Helen. "Tell me what happened and don't scrimp on the highlights. I love a good story."

"Well," she said, as if hesitant to begin, "Mrs. Littleword came into the library where I'd been working and introduced herself. She couldn't locate Mary, the receptionist, so I offered to help. We came down into the hall and found the man lying on the floor with his head bashed in."

"What about you, Mrs. Littleword?" Johns asked. "You've been in it today. A mugging in the market and now an attempted murder at The Grange. Maybe I ought to take you in and lock you up to bring the crime rate down," Johns said sourly.

Helen gave Martha an uncertain look.

Martha stiffened but ignored the verbal jab.

"Like she said, we came out looking for the receptionist and saw some type of liquid on the floor. Helen bent down and we realized it was blood. It was then I saw the man lying behind the desk. He wasn't there before."

"Before? Explain," Johns said.

"I came to The Grange intending to meet with Mr. Devry, the curator. I'm taking his statement in a case. I rang the bell on the desk and no one came, so I looked around to see if anyone was there. No one was here and certainly not someone with their head bashed and bloody."

"You two know each other?" Johns asked.

"No, this is the first time we've met," Martha said with a smile.

"Yes, that's right. We seem to have been thrown into a mess," Helen said with a short laugh.

It was John's turn to look quizzically at Helen. "You find this humorous, Mrs.?"

"Ryes. Helen Ryes. No, I...I...I'm feeling a bit overwhelmed," Helen stammered apologetically.

"You don't need to be so gruff with us. Helen is in shock!" Martha said hotly.

Johns was surprised by the redhead's sudden temper. She stood there defiantly looking at him, her blue eyes boring into his. He changed his tone to a softer one.

"I need both your statements. Where are you staying?" he asked.

Helen quickly looked at Martha and said, "I'm at the old pub on King's Street. I can't remember its name. Not much to pick from this time of year."

"True," Johns agreed as he scribbled something in his small notebook. "That place has seen better days. What about you, Mrs. Littleword?"

"I own Flower Pot Cottage on Canal Street. First house I've ever owned." Martha said with a hint of pride in her voice.

"Seems fitting," he grumbled while writing something in his notebook.

"What does that mean?" Martha asked again as if she was insulted by his comment.

Again, Johns was struck by the woman's feisty attitude. He chose not to take the bait but he couldn't help but wonder what the world was coming to. One woman was barely able to contain her laughter and the other was thinking about paint swatches for her new house while a man was bleeding to death not more than ten feet from them.

"Don't go anywhere. Police Constable Cross will take your statements. By the way," said Johns pointing at the man who was now on the gurney, "either of you ever seen the gent before?"

"No," both women answered in unison.

"I have," said a small voice.

Everyone turned to look at a pretty, young girl with black curly hair standing in the door staring at the man on the gurney.

"Mary!" Helen announced.

Johns turned toward the new arrival. "You there. Come here, please."

The girl came over to them, her big, round eyes darting looks at the man lying on a gurney.

"Young lady, what's your full name? I assume you are the receptionist?" Johns asked.

"I am," she said with a slight quiver to her voice. "My name is Mary Wilton. What happened here? Is Sir Carstons dead?"

"No, surprisingly he is still alive," Johns said with a sour look at Helen and Martha.

Helen flinched, but Martha returned his sour look.

The paramedics pushed the gurney out the entrance way.

"Everyone around here knows Sir Carstons and that he used to own The Grange," Johns said. "But he doesn't live here anymore, so do you have any idea what he was doing here today?"

"Right. It's odd he's here," Mary answered hesitantly, and then went on. "He's not supposed to be here. The Grange is in the hands of a board of trustees now. I was told to let Mr. Devry know if he ever visited. I've worked here for about three months, and I've only seen Sir Carstons once."

Johns jotted something down in his notebook and then asked, "Where have you been Miss Wilton? Do you usually take such long lunch breaks?"

"No, not usually. Today I took my break about two o'clock, but I had to stop at the post office so it took longer to get back," Mary explained.

"Looks like I need a statement from you, too, Miss Wilton. Police Constable Cross will take it."

Johns turned to go. He hoped Sir Carstons pulled through. Otherwise he would be in it thick. With so many tourists at this time of year, there wasn't any telling why Sir Carstons had been hammered.

"Ladies, we'll get your statements then you may go. I'll ask that you not touch anything. Thank you." Johns touched his forehead in a good-bye salutation and stiffly marched out of The Grange's old front doors leaving Helen, Martha and Mary quietly staring after him.

SCENE BREAK

"Good riddance," Martha said as Johns left through the front doors.

Helen turned to face Martha. "Don't like him much?"

"He didn't need to be so rude and he made me feel like we were guilty of popping Sir Carstons in the head."

"Sir Carstons," Helen said half to herself but looking at the other two.

"Yeah, I wonder what he was doing here," Mary said. "He isn't supposed to be on the property. He and the board are in it over something."

"Have you seen Mr. Devry today, Mary?" Martha asked. "I was supposed to meet him to take his statement."

"Oh, yeah, I remember talking with you on the phone. He was here but got a call from his mother. Something about her not feeling well." She looked around nervously. "I don't want to stay here by myself. Helen, are you staying?"

Helen saw the apprehension on the young girl's face but didn't want to stay any longer herself in case a homicidal maniac was on the loose. "Mary, I don't have any authority here but under the circumstances, it might not be a bad idea to call your board's president and tell him what happened. He'll want to know. I'll be in the library for at least another thirty minutes."

Mary, obviously forgetting Chief John's request not to touch anything, started toward the phone on the reception desk. The coagulated droplets of blood still on the floor stopped her dead. An expression of horror and a sudden limpness to her frame, spurred Helen and Martha to move fast to catch her before she fell. They lifted her over to the bench they'd previously occupied and lay her down along its length. Martha propped Mary's head on her lap while Helen laid the girl's knees across her own. Both older women patted and offered maternal words of encouragement to the younger.

Here they were again, on the bench.

"I need a drink," Helen sighed.

"Yes, and I wish I still smoked," Martha agreed.

Chapter 8

Dr. Coolidge, the Head Librarian for the Harvard Library, went through the new manuscripts and personal papers donated from the recently deceased socialite and poet, Amy Lowell. Miss Lowell had generously left the library her highly sought-after collection of Keatsiana and other notable nineteenth century authors. As he unwrapped each item, he jotted down its title, author, published date and its condition.

Being an historian first, Dr. Coolidge loved this part of his job. It was a privilege to touch and study up close such rare, priceless things. He compared it to an archaeologist's excitement when a rock slab rolls back from an ancient tomb. All your senses come alive and you breathe in the air of the past. For one extraordinary moment your consciousness knows only the wonder of what you behold. It was pure magic.

The last items he pulled from the bottom of the enormous crate were enclosed in a small box, separated from the other manuscripts and papers. He pulled out the box and placed it on his work table. It opened easily and he removed an extremely small and exquisitely hand-bound book.

He recognized it immediately as one of the tiny books the Brontës had co-written as children. Few of these rare jewels existed in the world and he was astonished to be holding one in his own hands.

With a sense of delighted anticipation, he reached in and felt for the last item in the chest. A leather box appeared. The leather was tooled in different Gothic Revival designs with a gold-embossed, quatrefoil center. Small brass hinges and an

31

ornate latch made up its hardware. The box was rosewood with the leather glued over and the hardware delicately mounted. It was either for holding stationary or family papers.

He lifted the lid and there was a manuscript without a cover of any kind. It was handwritten in a woman's hand. He quickly scanned the manuscript up to the last page where he noticed the penmanship became more awkward. Coolidge wondered, as he read the first chapter, if this manuscript might be an unfinished novel by one of the Brontës. There was a small poem written in a margin he would need to look into. He made a quick notation in his notebook, "hand-written manuscript, author unknown, date unknown but likely 1825 to 1850's, Amy Lowell collection, donated 1928."

Dr. Coolidge also accessioned the chest into his register. He did not return the manuscript or the tiny Brontë book to the chest but instead laid them both on clean cotton sheets on his work table. Feeling tired, he left his notebook open for Mildred, his assistant, to find in the morning. She would put the finishing touches on accessioning the Lowell collection.

When Mildred came in the next morning she went about her work and neatly typed all Dr. Coolidge's notes. She gingerly gathered each item of the collection, labeled them according to his notes, wrapped them in strips of cotton and put each in its own marked box.

The Brontë and the untitled manuscript were placed in separate boxes and delivered with the rest of Amy Lowell's collection to Harvard's special holding area for rare books and artifacts known as The Treasure Room. A more appropriate name could not have been coined for such a place.

Dr. Coolidge passed away early that same morning. The untitled manuscript he'd found among Amy Lowell's collection would sleep another seventy-five years until someone clever enough to recognize its worth would come along.

Chapter 9

Marsden-Lacey, England
Present Day

Mary revived fast. Youth always does Martha thought with a smile. They called Constable Cross to the door and asked if he could please take their statements soon. He was a nice looking, dark-haired young man and with one look at Mary's pretty but ashen face, he agreed to start.

After all three women finished their statements and Mary had permission from Piers Cousins, The Grange's Board President, to lock up early, Helen and Martha offered to walk Mary back to her flat but Constable Cross had already offered to drive the doe-eyed girl home.

Both women smiled understandingly at the two young people. The car pulled out of the car park leaving them standing together alone in the small entrance garden. The sun was setting over the Yorkshire countryside bringing that exquisite mixture of drowsiness and peacefulness to the summer landscape.

"How bout that drink?" Martha offered.

"Let's go. I know a great place," Helen said.

"Um, let's not go to The Kings Way, the place you're staying. I'm sorry, but that place is a dive. It doesn't really fit your style, if you don't mind me saying so," Martha said.

"You can say so. It's a dive but there were so many tourists this time of year, I couldn't find anywhere else. I've got to be here for at least three more days, so it has to be The Kings Way or nothing."

The two tired women made their way down the hill into the charming village of Marsden Lacey. At the peak of the tourist season, Marsden-Lacey attracted a variety of holiday-makers.

Families, hikers, and motorcyclists all came to enjoy the Yorkshire Dales National Park while others such as the boaters meandered in their motor crafts of choice through the canal.

It was a village of 12,000 souls during the off-season but in the later part of July, it swelled to over 15,000 on the weekends. The girls found their way down to one of the village's favorite watering holes, The Traveller's Inn.

"Let's go in here," Helen said.

They pushed though the door into the old fashioned but highly-sought-out local pub. Dark beams, small windows with chintz curtains, cozy booths and two working fireplaces made The Traveller's Inn the quintessential English hostelry. Tonight there was a dart tournament going on. Every so often there was an explosion of merry making and shouting from the back of the pub where the dart boards hung in a row.

Martha picked out a cushioned bench with a table near an open window overlooking the back garden. The air coming in smelled fresh with the scent from the lavender bushes planted below the window. They sat down with sighs and ordered two glasses of the house wine from the waitress.

"What a day," Martha said more to herself than to Helen.

"I guess so. You've been through it. Mugged in the market and a witness to a possible murder at The Grange."

Martha chuckled. "I must have brought some kind of weird mojo along with me when I entered The Grange. What do you suppose the whole thing was about?"

"Well, if you want my guess, I'd say it has something to do with what Mary said about the board and Sir Carstons being into it."

Martha looked thoughtful. "Had you ever met Sir Carstons or heard about him when they asked you to assess the collection?"

"No. I've only talked with Louis Devry, the curator, who seems stuffy but nice. Why does your firm need a statement from him?" Helen asked.

"I think it's going to make the news tomorrow anyway, so I might as well tell you. Sir Carstons is in the process of suing The

Grange's governing board. The board basically was a group of private individuals who entered into a financial arrangement with Sir Carstons to purchase The Grange based on a valuation that was compiled by an outside company. Sir Carstons is claiming the valuation was mismanaged because the firm that produced it turned out to be owned by a board member's nephew."

"Oh, boy. Messy, and I'm beginning to see why Louis Devry has been so insistent about the collection being assessed quickly," Helen said.

They sat quietly for a few seconds. An attractive man threaded his way through the customers and approached their table.

"Mrs. Littleword and Mrs. Ryes?" he said once he reached their table. "I'm Piers Cousins, The Grange's board president. May I sit down with you for a moment?"

Helen and Martha exchanged glances.

"Of course, Mr. Cousins, have a seat." Martha motioned for him to sit.

Piers Cousins stood close to six feet tall with a slim, athletic build. He was near fifty years old but his dark hair was only slightly greying at the temples. He had deep blue eyes and was extremely handsome.

With a quick glance to his left hand, Helen noted he wasn't wearing a wedding ring. There were other signs of his single state such as he wasn't wearing clothes wives typically picked for their husbands. The lack of tassels on his shoes was a clear indicator of no wife. He pulled up a chair from another table and sat down between the two women.

"I'm so sorry about what you both have been through today. It must have been a terrible shock," Cousins said in his lovely, aristocratic accent. "I've been over to check on The Grange and something is troubling me."

"Assaults are often troubling," Martha said impertinently.

Cousins, checked for an instant by Martha's sarcasm, gave her an amused look.

Helen took up the thread of the momentarily derailed conversation and asked with a touch more concern than sounded natural, "What is troubling you?"

The girls exchanged knowing looks.

"I walked through the entire building because I wanted to make certain nothing was amiss but also to be certain no one had hidden themselves inside. We do this every night because it's a public building and we worry about theft and vandalism," Cousins said.

While he was talking, Helen saw how well his hands were formed. Long fingers, bony but strong with nice nails told her he wasn't a fussy type but probably liked to work outside. The rest of his clothes said money but weren't pretentious in any way. As she studied him surreptitiously, she realized how nervous he was.

"Mr. Cousins, I can assure you the police and Mary did an excellent job of going over the entire property before we left," she said.

"I'm sure they did, but I thought that whilst you were going through the rooms you might have noticed something?"

"Like what?"

He hesitated then said, "The upstairs rooms look like a scuffle must have taken place. Fragile books displayed on top of counters inside glass cases were askew. I wondered if you might have heard anything or seen anyone?"

"No. Just a man bashed over the head lying in a pool of blood," Martha said with an impish smile.

Cousins, this time, gave her a slightly confused look. Martha shrugged.

"Oh. Mrs. Littleword, I'm being completely thoughtless," he said with a slight blush. "It's that I'm confused by this whole affair and wondered if you might have seen something. Especially you, Mrs. Ryes, with your detailed eye, might have noted an oddity or something misplaced." He turned toward the more empathetic one, Helen.

"Mr. Cousins, we understand this has been an upsetting experience for everyone," Helen said soothingly. She patted his hand lightly and shot a stern look toward Martha who rolled her eyes in response. "We've been through so much excitement today. Everyone's nerves are on edge."

"I apologize again, ladies. Let me make this up to you," he said penitently while casting an unsure look at Martha. "Tomorrow, The Grange Society will be having their annual fundraiser at my home, Healy House. It's a tennis tournament which we're proud to say is in its twelfth year. The matches start at nine a.m. and you are welcome to come as my guests. Please stay on afterward and have dinner, too, around seven. It's a casual affair and if you enjoy tennis, you will see some of the best players we English can boast of." The last bit was said with the true tennis enthusiast's excitement.

Helen and Martha said they would like to attend and exchanged phone numbers with Piers. As he left The Traveller's Inn, both women watched his retreating figure until it was lost among the throng of happy patrons.

"Why were you being so snippy with him?" Helen, slightly annoyed, turned to Martha.

"I just wanted to see what he would do. He might be the killer, Helen."

Helen stiffened.

Martha continued in a mock high-society voice. "Besides, we've been invited to the castle, my dear. Count your blessings. Sounds like we are going to have a lovely time."

Martha started laughing at her own silliness which infected Helen, too. Holding up her glass for Helen to toast along with her, Martha said, "To Healy House we go!"

As they clanked the glasses together, they couldn't help another giggle or two.

Chapter 10

The next day was Saturday and Helen woke up to yelling and pots banging in the kitchen below her room. She winced and pulled the blankets over her head, wishing she could find anywhere, absolutely anywhere else to stay. She couldn't wait to be done with the job at The Grange. The hotel was a mess, her life was even messier, and now she was a witness (maybe even a suspect) in an attempted murder investigation.

There had been one highlight to the whole affair. Well, maybe two, once she thought about it. She had enjoyed meeting Martha. Martha was definitely a quirky person but fun and not a push-over. And the other nice highlight was Piers Cousins.

Since rotten old George, her ex-husband, had chosen to regain his youth by running off with her assistant, Fiona, Helen's only focus was work. The last year had been about holding on to her half of the business and trying to not spend every waking moment wondering how life could go from wonderful to into the toilet in less than a week which was how long Fiona had been working for their business before George went feral.

It was all in the past, but she had to make a decision about his wedding. Why in the world had Fiona and George invited her to the wedding? It wasn't like George to rub salt in someone's wounds, but then if someone had asked her a year and a half ago if she thought her loving George would pop off with a girl almost the same age as their daughter, Helen would have laughed. She and George were best friends or so she'd thought.

With a heave and a flip of the blankets, Helen moved toward the place where her clothes were hanging in a recess behind the room's door. Today was a fresh start. After a quick choice of a white cardigan and blouse, pearls and a lavender, pleated, mid-length skirt, she went into the bath. Her spirit felt lighter than it had in ages, so she decided to look her best for her first visit to Mr. Cousins' Healy House.

Scene break

Flower Pot Cottage was nicely situated along Canal Street. It had a happy location across from the Huddleston Narrow Canal with a nice rock wall embankment and perfectly manicured hedges protecting it from any gawking hikers. There was no doubt in Martha's mind that it was worth every pound she'd paid for it.

After Kate, her only child, moved out, the cottage felt lonely. She and Gus, the cat, and Amos, the dog, wandered around the cottage for at least a month searching for something that wasn't coming back.

In time, they took themselves in hand and started fresh activities. Amos began a new project of watching "Dogs Who Work" episodes and barking at her canine sisters on canal boats floating past the cottage. Meanwhile, Gus kept her neighbor's pigeon coop under tight surveillance and Martha took self-defense and karate classes at the Village Community Center.

A clanking sound told Martha a fresh group of narrow boats were readying themselves to lower the water in the section of the canal outside her cottage. She'd lain in bed long enough this morning. Gently lifting herself from between the cat and dog so she didn't disturb their comfort, she maneuvered herself from the bed. With one last furious tug on her nightgown still entangled in the sheets, she finally extricated herself from her nest.

Sleep came late last night and wasn't extremely beneficial. If anything, it had been downright fitful and agitated. Mr. Cuthbirt, her boss, would be a sourpuss over Devry's statement not being taken. In the last six months, her work load at the law firm had nearly doubled from what it had been before. Things felt overwhelming and slightly out of control.

She reflected on her day ahead. The fundraiser at Healy House was going to be a real treat. Tennis and food, and of course mixing with the posh tennis people, would be so much fun.

Whatever she wore today, it had to be light and pretty. Martha got up and dug through the closet, finding a summery dress with a delicate floral pattern.

Gus and Amos blinked sleepily from the bed as they watched Martha fling things about and rifle through heavily packed drawers. Finally, their fearless leader laid her chosen outfit on the bed and hurried into the bath.

Amos watched the bathroom door close and got up stretching her gimpy hind legs and yawned. Then ceremoniously circled three times and plopped back down on top of Martha's lovely white and floral dress, falling happily asleep.

Chapter 11

The summer had been perfect. Warm days with gentle, playful breezes and the right amount of rain providing West Yorkshire with a summer so exquisite that few old folks could remember a better one.

If any place epitomized an English country house in its summer finery, it was Healy House. Originally built by a wealthy wool merchant in 1569, it exhibited all the best of Elizabethan architecture. A rambling, timber-framed house of twenty-three rooms and four clustered chimneys sat upon a rise in the land above the Calder River.

Flower boxes filled with ivies, pink fuchsias and white petunias festooned the house's front mullioned windows. Tall pines rearing their majestic heads on the hills behind the house added a sense of grace and peacefulness to the picture-postcard scene. The house and its environs either made visitors feel like the luckiest of souls to behold its charms or made them desperate to own it. Fortunately for Piers Cousins, its owner, the majority of his guests that day were of the former disposition.

It was Cousins' father, John Cousins, who was responsible for his son's immense wealth. He invented *Manly*, an aftershave made popular in the sixties and still in demand today. The senior Cousins had a brilliant business mind and landed on the idea of gifting his products to famous sports stars. By doing so, he became the father of the celebrity endorsement idea and it paid off nicely.

John Cousins bought Healy House and built four grass tennis courts with which he intended to host tournaments with world-renowned tennis pros benefiting both his pocket book and his business' brandname. Unfortunately for John Cousins, he died too young, leaving his estate to his seven-year-old son, Piers.

Once he came of age, Piers reinstated the yearly invitation-only, private tennis tournament as a legacy to his father.

When The Grange's board of directors invited Piers Cousins to be a member, he graciously offered the tennis tournament as a fundraiser for the new museum. The usually private tennis tournament was opened to well-healed, paying guests who could afford to mingle with tennis stars and other celebrities. The money generated from the event allowed The Grange's collection acquisition committee to focus on purchasing only the best works currently available in the world to buy. Needless to say, The Grange was creating quite a name for itself in the museum world community.

Once again this year, everything for the tournament was planned to perfection and even the weather was complying nicely. Celebrities were photographed arriving in Birmingham's airport with captions in gossip papers about how they were attending Healy's famed and exclusive tennis party. The media was always excited to add to the tournament's hype if it meant selling magazines and internet ads.

Tennis pros and their coaches arrived and were readying themselves for their matches. The public and press waited eagerly at the entrance gates to catch sight of the famous and the infamous. Dark-suited security officers patrolled the estate while caterers were busy managing the dining facilities within immense, white billowing tents.

Into this mix of who's who Martha and Helen arrived looking like typical summer lawn tennis spectators. With bright and curious expressions, they wandered around to the refreshment tents and partook of a glass of chardonnay and a bowl full of summer berries with clotted cream while surreptitiously eyeing the collection of glamorous attendees.

At the table, Martha's cell phone rang. The displayed number was the Marsden-Lacey's police station.

"This can't be good," she said to Helen as she answered the phone. "Hello, this is Martha Littleword speaking."

42

"Mrs. Littleword, DCI Johns, Marsden-Lacey Police. I'm letting you know that until further notice I'll need you and Mrs. Ryes to stay in contact with the station. You're potential suspects in a murder investigation."

"Murder?" Martha said a bit too loudly.

Helen's eyes flew open at the word and a blueberry almost escaped from her mouth due to her dropped jaw.

"That's right. Sir Carstons died in the hospital. I need to be able to keep close tabs on everyone involved. You found him, so stay in town for a while," Johns said. "Oh, yeah, I'll be getting in touch with your cohort, the Ryes woman, to tell her the same thing."

"Don't bother, Inspector. My cohort is right here. I'll tell her myself." Martha ended the call.

"He's dead, isn't he?" Helen said in a whispery voice.

Martha could see what was coming but Helen went on.

"Oh, my God. Sir Carstons is dead. What if we had done more? What if it's our fault he didn't make it?"

"Don't go there, Helen. It wasn't our fault and we did everything we were able to do. I wish Johns could see you right now, then he would be absolutely convinced that you aren't a murderer."

"What?" Helen hissed as people turned to look at them. "What do you mean 'convinced I'm not a murder?'"

People in the dining tent whispered to each other while throwing furtive glances at Martha and Helen.

"Okay, simmer down," Martha said in a firm but hushed voice. "He doesn't want us to leave the village for a short bit because we're potential suspects in a murder investigation. We need to stick around."

"I can't. I absolutely can't stay any longer. First, my reservation is almost up at the hotel from hell and I need to get back to Leeds to start work on some of these conservation jobs." Helen was taking the denial route.

Martha sat back in her chair and stirred the berries around in their cream with a silver spoon. "You know what? You can stay with me. I've got a dog and a cat, though. Some people don't like animals in a house but they're my kids now that Kate is at Oxford. I've got plenty of room and it's definitely quieter than The Kings Way."

Helen studied her new friend's face then looked down at her hands lying limply in her lap, and started to tear up. "I feel like things are so out of control, you know?"

Martha did see, and because she was a deeply nurturing soul, she wanted to make Helen's situation better somehow.

"Hey, it's not all that bad," she coaxed. "We'll have fun. Do you like pets?" She patted Helen's hand maternally.

"Yes, I do." Helen sniffled using her table napkin to dab her nose.

"Well, then, it's settled. You're staying with me until this thing is done and we can work something out with Chief Inspector Johns about your work in Leeds. He'll have to work with us somehow."

Martha picked up her purse and Helen dried her eyes. They meandered around the beautiful grounds of Healy House like two old friends visiting a pretty garden on their day off.

It was a fantasy land of natural and human-inspired beauty. Their spirits picked up and they found themselves laughing at Martha's story of her recent mugging in the market place by some teenager. They were having a good time for being murder suspects and even had high prospects for an enchanting evening with the handsome, eligible, and wealthy prince of Healy, Piers Cousins.

Chapter 12

Chief Inspector Johns sat in his chair at the police station. He was off duty so he reached into the bottom drawer of the file cabinet and pulled out a woman's purse. It was a nice, black number, discrete and something most women might have in their wardrobe. This made it a perfect place in a police chief's office to hide a bottle of Scotch whiskey. No one would ever look there.

He made a cup of black tea and added the whiskey. The phone rang and he grimaced. It was like the universe enjoyed messing with him some days.

He picked up the phone. "Johns, here," he said in a grumpy tone.

"Sergeant Cross here, Chief Inspector. We have the forensic reports on the Carstons' case. Looks like his head was smashed in by a blunt object and it had to be a good sized one. We didn't find anything the day of the attack on Sir Carstons that might have been the murder weapon. Should I go back again to The Grange and take a look around the garden?"

"Yeah, I'll meet you there in thirty minutes, Sergeant."

This was Marsden-Lacey's first murder in six years and young Sergeant Cross could barely contain his enthusiasm. It was like giving a kid his first bike, thought Johns as he swigged down the rest of his tea, grabbed two biscuits and stuffed them into his pocket. He wouldn't be having dinner anytime soon, and he wished Cross wasn't so gung-ho. It would have been nice to stop into The Traveller's Inn and get something to eat tonight. Lilly would be working.

When he arrived at The Grange, Sergeant Cross was already there and he signaled for Johns to join him by the rock wall overlooking the hillside toward the village.

"Eager beaver," Johns thought to himself.

"Okay, Cross, what have you found?" he asked.

"Sir, I think I should scramble down the side and take a look. We've scouted the entire area except this hillside. Since it's now a murder investigation, we might see if anything was tossed over. I waited for you to decide."

"Go ahead, son. If you find something, leave it. We'll need to call in forensics."

Ten minutes later, as Johns sat on the stone wall outside The Grange finishing his snacks and pondering the universe's sense of humor, Sergeant Cross called up jubilantly from the side of the hill.

"I found it, Sir! It's matted with blood!"

Johns looked down the slope. Sergeant Cross smiled up at him like a puppy who had fetched his first ball.

"Get yourself up here. I'm calling Thompson. His forensic team will take it from here."

Johns looked down the hill at the young man scrambling up towards him. He was a good kid and it had been nice for a change to work with someone who had a thrill for the job. Youthful enthusiasm could infect even a cynic like Johns.

"Cross, nice job and good instincts," Johns gruffly complimented the young detective.

"Thanks. Sir, there's one thing more. I saw a hefty-sized rock with blood on it, but something else was with it."

"Oh? What did you find?" Cross had Johns' full attention.

"There appears to be a piece of paper stuck to the rock or maybe a torn half of a check. I couldn't tell exactly," Cross said. "It may have stuck to it as it rolled down the hill, but I thought it might be of importance."

"Could you make anything out on it?"

"Yes, Sir. It had a name. It said 'Cousins.'"

Scene Break

Helen and Martha were enjoying their tea time in one of the open dining tents when Helen's mobile rang.

"Hello," she said.

"Mrs. Ryes? Hello, this is Piers Cousins. I want to offer you and Mrs. Littleword one of my guest rooms to rest in and refresh yourselves before dinner. If you will come round by the small garden door, my housekeeper, Mrs. Thyme will show you to your room."

Helen smiled showing a dimple in her right cheek.

"Oh thank you. That would be lovely."

She ended the call. "Looks like there's another treat in store for us today. Piers Cousins offered us a room to rest in until dinner. Follow me."

It was hard to suppress the excitement of seeing inside such a wonderful house. They made their way to the house's west side but once they reached the door, Helen came to an abrupt stop. Waiting to let himself through the gate was Mr. Louis Devry, The Grange's curator.

"Mr. Devry? Hello," Helen said, surprised at seeing the missing curator.

"Mrs. Ryes, hello. How are you this afternoon? You must be attending Piers' dinner tonight, too. It's always wonderful to be at Healy," Devry said with a warm smile.

Louis Devry stood six feet tall and weighed about 190 pounds. His sandy blond hair was trimmed short in a conventional manner for men and he looked to be in his mid-forties.

He had the accent of an Englishman who had spent a good deal of his young life in America probably near Boston. He was dressed in a light summer suit of grey with simple dark loafers and no wedding ring. On the whole, he was a pleasant-looking man who looked over-tired and slightly worried.

"I'm so sorry, Mr. Devry, but have you been made aware of the terrible incident which happened yesterday at The Grange?" Helen asked.

"No, I'm sorry I had to leave yesterday in a hurry. A care nurse telephoned from Oxton saying my mother was ill. I went to her immediately."

"Oh, I'm sorry to hear that and I hope she's doing better," Helen replied then pushed on. "Mr. Devry, I feel I need to tell you there was a terrible attack on Sir Alan Carstons. He was found senseless. Someone hit him in the head. The police came and he was taken to the hospital. He...died."

Louis Devry blinked at her like he couldn't take in what she'd said. Without responding to her, he instead leaned back against the rock wall and took his handkerchief from his trouser pocket. He wiped his forehead and flushed visibly.

"Are you okay, Mr. Devry?" Helen asked.

"Oh, Mrs. Ryes," he said breathlessly. "How did it happen?"

Helen glanced quickly at Martha who raised her eyebrows and shrugged slightly as if to say, "Go ahead but I'm glad it's you and not me."

"No one knows exactly what happened but someone hit him from behind. He didn't regain consciousness at the hospital. Maybe someone was trying to rob the museum. The police will probably want to talk with you," Helen finished.

"Of course." The exhaustion in Devry's face intensified and he was looking unwell.

Martha, who had been fiddling with the gate's latch, finally worked the mechanism and the gate swung open. Helen and Louis Devry followed her into the small, walled garden.

Turning to Devry, she said, "Mr. Devry, my name is Martha Littleword. I was supposed to meet with you yesterday to take your statement. I'm with Partridge, Sims and Cuthbirt."

"Yes, Mrs. Littleword. I am so sorry. Mary wasn't around and once I got the call from my mother, everything else went out of my mind. Would tomorrow be okay to try again?"

"Yes, thank you. Would three o'clock be convenient?"

"I think that will work fine," Devry replied. This last bit was said with a vagueness which didn't inspire confidence in his remembering the next meeting any better than he had the first.

They reached the flagstone patio to the rear of the house and pulled the bell chain hanging beside a wide set of French doors. A small, bright-eyed woman with a perfectly white apron opened the door.

"Louis. How are you? It is so good to see you again," she said with warmth and obvious joy at seeing an old, much-loved visitor to Healy. Then looking at Helen and Martha, she gave them a big smile, "And you must be the guests Mr. Cousins told me about. I'm Mrs. Thyme, Mr. Cousins' housekeeper. Follow me and I'll show you your rooms."

They'd been let into the back of the house along a corridor flanked on one side by ornate, multi-paned clear windows and honey-colored, oak-paneled walls on the other. The sunlight dappled across the flagstone floors and made shadows dance along the passageway. Soft tones of green coming in from the garden gave the space a feeling of peacefulness and timelessness.

Too soon, they came to a low door which opened into the main hall. Mrs. Thyme gestured for the group to follow her up the stairs. She merrily chatted about the day's excitement and the number of famous people staying in the house.

Louis Devry was shown his room where he said good-bye to Martha and Helen, promising to see them later at the dinner. The girls followed Mrs. Thyme to the end of the hallway. There, she opened the door into a charming bedroom.

Two mahogany twin beds sat side by side, each with canopies made from a rose-patterned chintz fabric. In between the beds lived a small Sheridan night stand with an exquisite brass student's lamp sporting a green shade. The old oak beams of the room were blackened with age and stood out in contrast to the plaster of the walls which was painted a simple, fresh butter color.

Every comfort had been considered by their host. Bottles of water and a tin of chocolates were placed on the night stand with a small, delicately-printed card which read:

"Stranger, what e'er thy land or creed or race,
Here rest awhile, there's virtue in the place." -
Anonymous

A beautiful bouquet of fresh, summer flowers had been placed on a round cherry-wood table and a basket full of toiletries sat on a lady's dressing table.

Martha moved toward the open windows. A gentle breeze lifted her hair as she pulled aside the lace curtains and looked out onto the manicured lawn which stretched down to the river and the pastures beyond.

Mrs. Thyme showed them the adjoining bath then reminded them that dinner would be served at eight but cocktails started at seven. She let herself out and with a soft click of the door, left Helen and Martha alone.

"Does this place give you an oddly wonderful feeling?" Helen asked.

They could hear the cheers from the tennis matches still taking place, but the sound was muffled by the distance between the house and the courts. There was an unspeakable pleasantness and peace that came from relaxing in such a delightful room.

"Yes it does," Martha said in a slow, lazy way as she sat down on one of the beds and fiddled with trying to open one of the chocolate tins. "It's like I have slipped off into a happy dream and I don't want to wake up."

Helen watched Martha flip her shoes across the room. "I know. It's almost as if you've taken some kind of tranquilizer and everything is how it's supposed to be. I get the feeling some people might do whatever it takes to wrangle an invitation to Healy."

"I think," Martha replied as she popped one of the chocolates from the opened tin into her mouth and stretched out on the soft bed, wriggling her bare toes, "that some people might take it further than an invitation, Helen. I think some people might even commit murder to have Healy House be their home."

Chapter 13

It was later after their rest and the chocolate tin was nearly empty Martha realized she'd left her dress shoes in her car. As she made her way down the staircase, she saw Louis Devry with a manila envelope under his arm walking into one of the rooms off the main hall.

Martha was an avid visitor of historic homes, but the lure of sneaking a glance into some of Healy's rooms made her want to follow Devry. If he stopped, she could always offer a nice "Hello," and it would seem as if she weren't being a tourist, but friendly.

Approaching the doorway, she realized it must be Piers Cousins' study. Through the half-opened door, she saw a massive, mahogany desk piled with papers and heard Cousins' voice, sharp with irritation.

Instinct made her hesitate. Instead of continuing into the room, she looked up and down the hall to see if anyone was around and then secreted herself into the doorway's alcove. She turned her full attention onto the conversation happening in the study. Piers was talking with Louis Devry about Sir Carstons' death. At first his voice was muffled, then, in a louder voice, she heard Piers say, "He was such a vicious bastard, Louis. I'm glad he's dead. Now maybe I'll be able to get somewhere with my suit."

Martha's body stiffened at his vehemence. She leaned in closer to hear better.

"Yes, he was the worst kind of bully. Women and children were Carstons' favorite prey. No one would have liked to see him dead more than me," Louis Devry said.

Martha heard a door open down the hall and she jumped back into the corridor as Mrs. Thyme bustled around the corner.

"Oh, Mrs. Littleword. I nearly ran you down," a flustered Mrs. Thyme said.

"I came down to get my shoes from my car," Martha said acutely aware of the squeakiness of her voice. "It might take me some time to walk over to the car park. Will it be okay if I let myself in through the garden again?"

"Oh, I'm so busy with everything there is to do by tonight, I can barely keep my wits about me. You help yourself, dear." Mrs. Thyme hurried off down the corridor.

In due time, Martha made her way into the sunlight of the garden and took a deep breath. "You almost landed yourself in a mess that time, Martha," she mumbled out loud.

During their day enjoying Healy's tournament, Helen and Martha had speculated on who wanted Sir Carstons dead and why. A burglary no longer seemed logical because nothing was taken from the museum. Carstons was found with his wallet and his Rolex on his arm. Whoever smashed in Sir Carstons' head didn't want quick cash.

Healy's car park was a ten-minute walk and the summer sun hovered along the horizon. Looking around to make sure no one noticed her muttering to herself, she continued musing on what she'd heard Piers and Louis talking about.

Both definitely disliked Sir Carstons. The law firm Martha was working for was involved in a suit involving The Grange's board and Sir Carstons. Could that be the suit Piers Cousins was referring to? If Sir Carstons was out of the picture, maybe the suit was void. From reading the other statements in the brief, she knew Sir Carstons was making life difficult for The Grange's board of directors and there were some sticky financial problems the museum inherited because of Sir Carstons' earlier poor fiscal management.

Then there was Devry's comment about Carstons being a bully. Louis Devry, from first appearances, seemed the reserved gentleman-type, but he obviously hated Carstons with a passion, too. The part about women and children being Carstons' favorite prey was an interesting thing to say. Martha wrinkled her nose at the thought of some body bullying the weak.

After she collected her shoes from her car and was making her way back to the house, Martha saw one of Marsden-Lacey's police vehicles coming along the drive. DCI Johns pulled up and got out at the front gate. Sergeant Cross followed him and Mrs. Thyme let them into the house.

Martha turned up her speed and slipped through the back gate. She called Helen on her cell phone.

"Hello," a sleepy Helen answered.

"Helen, get downstairs. Johns is here and he's in the house. I think something's up. Meet me at the foot of the staircase. Pronto."

"You bet. I'll be there."

Martha hustled into the hall and there was Chief Johns and his sergeant waiting to be shown into see Piers. She knew they would be waiting a while. She scanned the staircase and saw Helen making her way down. Martha continued up the hall and walked by the door to Piers' study again secreting herself into the alcove behind the door. Helen slipped over and squeezed in beside her.

Peeking between the door and the jamb into the study, she saw something that almost made her gasp out loud. Piers had walked over to one of the bookshelves and pulled on a piece of the framing. A section of the book shelving swung free and revealed a hidden passage. The entire house must have secret passages, Martha thought. Excited by this, she filed the information away to tell Helen later.

Mrs. Thyme walked right past Helen and Martha, never seeing them. She announced the chief and his sergeant to Piers. Johns walked into the room with Sergeant Cross in tow and flashed his badge.

"Mr. Cousins, I need to know your whereabouts yesterday," he said, getting right to the point of his visit.

"I was here most of the day getting things settled for the tournament and fundraiser. Mrs. Thyme might have some input.

At some point yesterday, my feet touched almost every foot of this estate. So many details to finish up," Cousins said.

"Would you know of anyone who might have been angry with Sir Carstons?" Johns asked.

"I thought you were treating this as an attempted burglary or something?"

"Well, Sir, are you aware of anything being stolen? If not and since we have a dead man, we're treating it as the 'something' and in this case, that's definitely murder," Johns said with a hint of challenge in his voice.

Piers studied the Chief briefly then replied with sincerity, "Well, to be honest Chief Inspector, you won't find too many people who didn't have a problem with Sir Carstons."

Louis Devry who'd been standing quietly beside Cousins, stepped forward and offered his hand. "Chief Inspector, I'm Louis Devry, the curator at The Grange. I think you'll probably want to talk with me about yesterday."

Johns raised his eyebrows. "The missing curator. I'll tell you what, gentlemen, let's take both your statements. I promise to be quick. I wouldn't want to hold up your dinner guests."

Piers motioned for the men to sit down. As Mrs. Thyme left the room, she closed the door, but not before Helen and Martha slipped out of their hiding place and made their way to the main hall.

"What do you think of that?" Helen whispered. "I think it's odd they're questioning Mr. Cousins, don't you?"

"Um, maybe not. I overheard him talking to Mr. Devry earlier and Cousins hated Sir Carstons. He had a grudge against him. One thing's for sure, the statement I'm supposed to get from Louis Devry is necessary in a suit The Grange's board brought against Sir Carstons. So when you think about it, the problem is no longer a problem, if you get my drift?"

"Cousins, a murderer? A squabble among board members and a disgruntled owner doesn't seem like a reason to kill someone," Helen said.

"Yeah, but, people have killed for less. There may be other motivations we aren't aware of…yet," Martha said with a twinge of drama in her voice.

"What are you getting at?" Helen nervously whispered.

"Might be a good idea to keep our eyes and ears open. Maybe there's a crazy person running around and someone else might get the hammer next," Martha said a little too enthusiastically.

"I think the only crazy person running around here is you and I'm not getting involved. Let the police handle it. They're the professionals."

Martha made a "pphht" sound.

"Piers Cousins isn't a killer," Helen said. "He's such a perfect gentleman."

"A little too perfect," Martha said. "Don't come crying to me if he's the killer. I promise not to say I told you so."

"How generous of you." Helen said with a sniff.

They found their way to a seating area and sat in wingback chairs covered with intricate, crewel-stitched fabric until DCI Johns and the others emerged from Cousins' office. The men appeared to be unaware of the two sets of eyes watching them intently.

"I'll need both of you to keep me informed if you need to leave Marsden-Lacey until I say otherwise," Johns was saying. "We're treating this as a murder investigation now. I've got forensics looking at the murder weapon and we'll be able to go through the security videos once Mr. Cousins delivers them to us Monday. Thank you, gentlemen, and I'll talk with you soon."

Martha noticed both Cousins and Devry looked anxious and tired. Louis Devry's face showed more strain than earlier. He excused himself and headed to his room upstairs. Cousins came over to Helen and Martha and sat down.

He wove a piece of card stock between his fingers.

"Is everything alright, Mr. Cousins?" Helen noticed his nervous behavior begin to slow down.

He looked at the card in his hand and slumped. "Please, call me Piers." He took a deep breath and let it out fast. "They've found some incriminating evidence against me. The weapon used to kill Carstons was one of the door stops we keep at the reception area. It was found chucked over the wall of the front entrance garden. A piece of one of my business cards was stuck to it." Cousins winced then continued. "Sir Carstons' blood was the glue holding it in place. A grisly indictment."

Then he added, "While we were in giving our statements, I remembered to tell Chief Johns that only last week we'd installed a few new security cameras at The Grange. I'm hoping they may have caught something or someone. It may save my neck anyway. I seem to be their prime suspect."

"You and Helen," Martha teased with an impish grin.

Piers looked back and forth between the two women.

Helen grimaced. "Martha and I were also asked not to change our location for a while. Chief Inspector Johns can be persuasive."

The main door opened and one of the tennis pros, Andy Burns, walked in. Seeing Piers he called out to him. Piers rose from his chair.

"Let's put this aside for the evening," he said. "I'm sure it will work out. When you're ready, please come down to the walled garden. We'll be dining al fresco tonight. It'll be a perfect night for it."

Cousins excused himself and Helen and Martha returned to their room. Soon, the lights on the tennis lawns went down. The girls were enjoying their pretty room. They took showers, worked on their hair and shared stories about their childhoods in Arkansas. When they heard people laughing and talking along the corridors, they checked the time and made their way down the stairs to the dinner party.

A slim crescent moon appeared over the tops of the old oak trees along the silvery, languid river. The balmy, summer night air lightly ruffled Helen and Martha's hair as they entered the fairy-land garden their host had imagined and prepared for his dinner guests. Strands of tiny white lights and hanging lanterns created a delicate canopy stretching across the entire stone wall enclosure.

Every round dining table was laid with pure white china dinnerware, silver cutlery, white linens, crystal stemware, centerpieces of fresh summer flowers, and long, tapered candles flickering inside glass hurricanes. Roses and gardenia plants planted in beds along the stone walls perfumed the evening air and soon laughing guests were sipping champagne and basking in the beauty of Healy House dressed to her finest.

Everyone, including Helen and Martha, who filtered into the area marveled at the enchanted garden. As if on cue, a string quintet accompanied by a piano began to play "Some Enchanted Evening." It appeared to be the beginning of a night to remember.

Chapter 14

The party was going wonderfully. Dinner was delicious and people were dancing to music by Sinatra, Nat King Cole and Perry Como. Helen and Martha were talking with Andy Burns, the tennis pro. He'd recently won his fifth tennis open and, out of friendship with Piers, flew all the way from Australia to play at Healy for the fundraiser.

The girls met his beautiful wife, Alex, a tall blonde who graced some of the more famous fashion magazines the world could boast of. Though she made her living wearing things beyond most women's reach, she told Helen she was more comfortable going barefoot in yoga pants and donning one of Andy's old t-shirt than having to dress up. Half-way through the evening, she was true to her word, when she removed her shoes and danced barefoot with her adoring husband. Beauty has its privileges Martha thought with a smile as she watched the young, handsome couple laughing and enjoying each other's company.

"Helen, may I have this dance?" Piers asked as the musicians began to play "Red Sails in the Sunset."

With a soft blush, Helen accepted and Martha gave her a "go have fun" wink as the couple moved onto the dance floor.

Martha decided to find the ladies' room. The windowed-hallway flanking the garden was softly lit by candles in sconces, and people half in shadow came and went along its length. Lightheaded from all the champagne, Martha walked into the main hall and as she passed Piers' study, she thought she saw a movement. Stopping abruptly, she strained to see if there was someone moving in the room's darkness. With only candles lighting the hall, it was difficult to tell.

With her curiosity on red alert, she peeked around the corner of the door to see a silhouetted form sitting in front of an illuminated computer screen. From her position she couldn't tell if it was a man or not. The person was frantically typing something into a white box which kept coming up on the screen. Each time it reappeared, they would try again.

As she watched, Martha leaned on the door and it creaked. The figure spun around and moved away from the desk. Quickly backing out of the doorway, Martha dashed for the stairs.

She heard people coming. Two women in evening gowns moved languidly down the hall, laughing. They stopped directly in front of the office. The person in the study was blocked from leaving. Martha decided not to go up the stairs. Instead, she walked past the women, down the long glass corridor, and back to the garden. With her fuzzy headedness gone from the need to be alert and quick, she decided the ladies room would have to wait.

Back in the garden, Helen and Piers were sitting at a table laughing cozily together. Martha worked her way through the crowd over to where they sat.

"Mr. Cousins, I think someone is in your study on your computer. I saw them when I was going up to my room."

Piers' got up and the two women followed him. Switching on the study's light, they discovered the office in a terrible mess.

"Who would have done this?" Piers asked, turning to Helen and Martha.

"I couldn't tell. They were on the computer," Martha said looking around. "Is anything is gone?"

"What do you think they were looking for?" Helen asked.

Piers searched through his desk then sat down in front of his computer. "Honestly, I can't tell much from fiddling with this thing. Nothing of value is gone from my desk." He swiveled slowly to face them. "I keep everything important in my safe which hasn't been touched. If our intruder wanted something, it must have been access to my computer and that could be devastating. I don't want the police out here again tonight but I don't think I have a choice."

"Piers, don't touch anything. Fingerprints could be on things," Martha warned.

At that moment a tall, thin strawberry blonde woman with an extremely clingy, silver-beaded evening gown leaned into the room. Her cleavage was a better accessory than a diamond necklace. In fact if she had been wearing the Hope diamond, no one would have noticed it.

She gave Piers a cute, pouty look and with her curled index finger she motioned for him to come. "Piers," she cooed in a deep Louisiana drawl, "I think the last dance is about to start. You know how I love to…dance, darling."

Martha turned from the strawberry blonde to look at Piers. Then, like a man whose will was controlled by a power greater than his own, he excused himself politely, saying he'd promised Lana the last dance.

Taking his arm in hers, Lana laid her head gently on his shoulder and they left the room.

Alone in the room, the girls were quiet for a few seconds until Martha said, "Whoa! I feel like I just witnessed the mating ritual of a Louisiana cougar."

Helen turned to Martha and said hotly, "Cougar is right. What's the deal with so many Americans in England these days? Don't they have better places to be?"

Martha laughed. "Now simmer down. We're Americans. Remember? You were outflanked by a Louisiana woman. Almost anyone would be caught by one of those molasses-dripping accents and those ta-tas. If I was mesmerized, you can damn well bet a man would be."

Helen laughed, too. "You know what? You're a goofball."

"Come on, let's go see what she's up to out on the dance floor with Piers. You've got as good a chance with posh boy as she does."

"What makes you think I even care?"

"Oh, for goodness sake, Helen. I saw your face when I walked into the garden a moment ago. Our Mr. Cousins is quite handsome but give yourself some credit, you're a looker, too. Don't let the Lana from Louisiana worry you."

Thanks. I think," Helen said sounding a bit uncertain.

"He's a nice person, Helen. At first I wasn't sure about him, but if he's our killer, he's a charming one. Seems almost as nice as my husband, Martin."

"Did you suspect your husband of being a killer, too?" Helen said with a smile.

"No, but he was a charmer though."

"Was? Are you not together anymore?"

"Not anymore. Martin died five years ago. He had cancer. I don't want to talk about that." Martha shook her head. "Instead, let me tell you how we met. Being just out of college, I'd come over to England to backpack with a friend over Christmas break. My friend, Holly, and I were sitting in Trafalgar Square one night feeling homesick and wondering why we'd ever wanted to come to England for Christmas, when I saw the most beautiful man I'd ever seen. He was wearing a long grey overcoat, had a tie and a vest, and he was dark-haired. I love dark-haired men."

Martha, on a roll, continued. "Unfortunately, Holly saw him at the same time. She was the better looking of the two of us. I don't know what got into me, but I decided within ten-seconds I wanted to meet him. I hopped down and walked up to him. He looked so surprised. Probably thought I was a prostitute, but I gave him a big smile and asked him in my sweetest voice if he could direct us to the perfect English pub. I told him my friend and I wanted to have dinner but didn't know where to go."

"Brazen hussy." Helen laughed.

"It worked, though, because once he smiled, I knew he was the one. It was the best Christmas present I ever received except when Kate was born. I know it sounds corny but it happened that way. Something clicked between us and it took cancer to separate us. Well, for the time being anyway." Martha smiled. "I'm saying if you like Piers, and I think you do, don't be afraid to throw your hat into the ring."

"Thanks, pal." Helen gave Martha a big hug. "Let's go check out the competition."

The girls started toward the garden when they heard a loud explosion arresting their forward motion to dead in their tracks.

All pandemonium broke loose. Women screamed and men's voices were yelling for people to get back. Guests came running down the hall with terrified expressions and someone called loudly for a doctor. The girls were unable to move while the tide of frightened people streamed down the long corridor around them.

Up ahead they saw the lovely Lana hurrying toward them. She grabbed Martha like she'd found a boulder in the stream to cling to. Wild-eyed and with blood splashed across her lovely dress, she held tightly to Martha.

Helen pulled the two women out of the current of humanity and over along the corridor's edge. She took Lana by the shoulders and, looking into her eyes, she gently asked her, "What is it, Lana? What's happened?"

"He's been shot," Lana cried in a strained voice. "Piers has been shot and the bullet grazed my arm. I think he's dead."

Chapter 15

After getting Lana settled on a sofa beside another woman who said she would keep an eye on her, Martha and Helen rushed back to the garden. Most of the guests had fled the area, but for a few people, and one man in his early thirties was bent over Piers.

Martha and Helen pushed their way into the small circle of people surrounding Piers.

"Are you a doctor?" Helen asked in a fearful but hopeful voice.

"Yes. I am," he said calmly.

"Will he be okay?"

"He's been shot in the upper shoulder. We've called and the ambulance is on its way. He's losing a lot of blood."

They watched as he continued his ministrations. Martha felt she must do something.

"Did anyone see who shot him?" She looked around at the guests left in the garden.

A man stepped forward and, in a German accent, said, "The shot came from over there." He pointed to a section of the garden's rock wall cast now in shadows.

Martha realized there was something unusual about its formation. Leaving the huddled group, she crossed over to get a better look at the spot indicated by the German guest.

Built into the wall was a perfectly round circle which opened upon the extensive lawn beyond. During the day it would be a lovely framed vista for garden visitors to look through, but if you were intent on killing someone, it made a perfect place to shoot someone without being seen.

One thing was for certain, Martha hadn't noticed the circle in the wall during the night's entertainment because of the intimate lighting, so whoever shot Piers was familiar with Healy House enough to know about the opening.

Finally, sirens whined their way up the road to Healy. The young doctor who'd been keeping watch over Piers gave way to the paramedics and watched over their efforts.

Within ten minutes a second set of sirens pushed their way toward Healy and shortly afterward, a rumpled DCI Johns stomped into the garden. His mouth was in a grim hard line and his hair was more rigid than ever.

Paramedics placed Piers on the gurney and into the ambulance. They left Healy at breakneck speed. Johns, took command of the area like a hard-nosed general barking orders and sending out officers to wrangle all the guests into the main hall. With people hustled from the garden like sheep, the Chief turned his attention to the crime scene. His officers cordoned off the area and were waiting for Johns to address the guests.

"I'll need everyone to stay put for a while until we do some interviewing and some forensic tests," Johns said to the fifty or so people huddled together looking worried and in shock. "Start bagging people's hands, sergeant. Make sure you don't miss a soul."

Scene Break

Two hours after the ambulance had left with Piers, the police were still busy interviewing the guests. Johns commandeered a sitting room as his special place to do interviews and Mrs. Thyme, the housekeeper, was his current prey. In his estimation though, she wasn't playing fair because all she was able to do was sniffle, cry and occasionally babble incoherently into her handkerchief.

"I'll need your full name, please, for the statement, and your position here," Johns said.

"Mrs. Hilda Thyme and I'm the housekeeper for Mr. Cousins."

64

"Mrs. Thyme, how many guests were invited to the dinner party?"

"I think it was sixty but not everyone could make it, you see?"

She looked up at him in a way as if to ask if he did see.

Unfortunately for Johns, he didn't see anything at that moment but the heavy, mahogany door gently opening and a bunch of red hair poking around the door's edge.

"Who's there?" he called out irritated that someone would interrupt his interview. His officers knew better.

"Um, Chief Inspector, it's me, Martha Littleword."

"Oh, my God. Are you here, too?" Johns said incredulously. "Mrs. Littleword, do you attend every violent criminal act in this village?"

"Yes. I mean, no," Martha returned, her tone indignant at the end. "I might be able to offer you some help, though, if you would try and be a little nicer."

She'd put her left hand on her hip.

Johns' blood pressure began to rise. What was the connection between this woman and all the disasters unleashed on Marsden-Lacey in the last forty-eight hours?

Remembering to try and be polite, his professionalism returned with a great force of effort. "I'm interviewing Mrs. Thyme at the moment. Could it wait…until your turn?"

Martha didn't move but instead leveled her own gaze onto the Chief's face.

"Your questioning might be improved by hearing what I have to say."

Chief Detective Inspector Merriam Johns wasn't used to having his authority questioned. For a moment neither broke their eye contact.

"What did you see, Mrs. Littleword?"

"There was someone in Piers' office earlier this evening. Whoever it was had rifled through his desk and I came in on

65

them. It was dark so I couldn't see who it was but possibly it was the murderer," Martha said with a glint of excitement in her eyes.

"Are you referring to Sir Carstons' murder because Cousins isn't dead...yet."

"Sir Carstons of course. I believe Piers will be fine." Martha turned to leave.

Johns dismissed people not the other way around.

"What makes you think it was the murderer, Mrs. Littleword? With this crowd it could have been someone trying to lift something. Probably knew Cousins was a wealthy man and wanted to take home their own version of a memento of the evening."

Martha pulled back from the door. "I think the person was trying to access Piers' computer for some reason."

Johns turned to his sergeant. "Cross, get the forensic team into Cousin's office. Go through it and yell if you find anything important."

"As for you, Mrs. Littleword, thank you for your information and by the way, where were you when Cousins was shot?" Johns asked. His tone implied he was digging at her a bit.

As cool as a cucumber, Martha replied, "I was in the main hall with Helen."

"Helen Ryes? Okay," he said looking down at his shoes and shaking his head. "I want both of you to meet me in Cousins' office in ten minutes. Thank you, Mrs. Littleword. This may be very helpful."

Then he stood up and bellowed, "Cross! Where is Cross? I need a strong cup of tea and has anybody got an aspirin?"

Martha held up her index finger. "I do," she said. "It's probably in my purse. I'll be happy to get it."

Johns stood there looking at her like she was an oddity of nature but he managed a simple grunt and a thank you. He turned to Mrs. Thyme and thanked her for her statement, dismissing her. The weeping housekeeper left the room and Johns called the sergeant to send in another person he could interview. He'd forgotten Martha's offer completely.

Scene Break

After leaving the library, Martha wondered why in the world she going out of her way to get an aspirin for that bad-tempered grump? As each person came out of the interview with Johns, she and Helen had listened to what they'd said about the kind of questions they were being asked inside. Martha, being a paralegal, knew how important it was to ask the right questions. Only she and Helen were aware of this bit of information and they were slated to be almost last in line. If Johns knew about the intruder in the study, he would be able to get farther in his investigation. She felt it was her duty to tell him before he missed the opportunity with the remaining guests.

The odd thing was how being in Johns' presence made her feel giddy and annoyed. He was an attractive man, to be sure, but he was also incredibly arrogant. Martha shook her head trying to sweep her thoughts away. Better get the aspirin and try not to think too much about it, she thought. The whole evening had been so intense. Maybe everything was finally catching up with her

The way to her room was lit with low lights. Soft moonlight coming in from the multi-paned window near the end of the hallway helped her to find her bedroom door. Letting herself in, Martha turned on the small electric hurricane lamp by the chair. The aspirin were in her purse so she grabbed the bottle and let herself back out of the room.

A soft breeze came gently down the hallway from the open windows bringing with it the scent of lavender and gardenia. As Martha reached the top of the stairwell, suddenly a strong push on her back hurled her downwards. The last thing she remembered was falling. Then pain and darkness.

Chapter 16

"Martha, are you okay? Martha, can you hear me?"

Martha could hear a man's voice but her eyes didn't want to open to see who it belonged to. Then the terrible headache swam up into her consciousness. Her throbbing head was all her mind was able to process at first, but slowly she remembered falling.

With a great effort, she lifted her eyes open and the first face she saw was DCI Johns'. He leaned over her with his face close to hers. Giddiness again fluttered up into her stomach, but then pain tore through her head, causing her to wince and shut her eyes.

"Can you hear me, Martha?" he asked gently.

His voice reminded her of Martin's when he'd been concerned. She tried to form words but all the air had been sucked out of her lungs. Pain in her arm and a sudden fear of not being able to breath started panic spreading throughout her brain. She shut her eyes and heard people clamoring about on the stairs. The vibrations from their movements melded with the hammering in her head.

"What happened?" a worried woman's voice asked. Martha thought it sounded like Helen's. The voice was slipping away and Martha willed herself to stay conscious.

"She's taken a tumble down the stairs," Johns said.

"Martha? She seems as sure-footed as a goat."

Martha flinched at the comparison.

"Oh, she must be in pain. See how she screwed up her face right then. We need to get a doctor in here. I'll go look for him. Keep her comfortable." Helen's voice receded from the room.

"Martha, try and open your eyes," Johns said coaxingly. His tone kind and almost tender.

With every physical effort available to her, she lifted her eyelids with a flutter and Johns' concerned face swam into focus. He was so close, so excitingly close. Martha lifted up her arm and touched his chest, he looked down. He stared at her hand, as she weakly opened it. There in her palm were the aspirins she had gone to get for him. Her hand dropped and she lost consciousness again.

Scene Break

"If you want my honest opinion, I think she needs to be in hospital tonight," the young doctor said after evaluating Martha who was now lying on the sofa in the library.

It was now past twelve-o'clock midnight. The house was quieting down and most of the guests departed after their statements or went upstairs to bed.

"I'm fine. I want to go home and rest," Martha said rubbing her temples.

"Martha, you need to be completely checked out to make sure nothing is wrong," Helen said putting special emphasis on the word "wrong" and pointing repeatedly at her own head.

"Helen, I get the point, but nothing is broken. My head can be checked out tomorrow. All I want is some sleep."

"I think it would be best if she didn't move much. Would it be possible for her to rest here tonight, Mrs. Thyme?" the doctor asked.

"Oh, of course she's perfectly welcome to stay here tonight," Mrs. Thyme said in a worried tone. "There are a few other guests staying on even after everything that's happened. Mrs. Ryes, would you be staying tonight as well?"

"If it wouldn't be any trouble. I'll be able to keep a good eye on her tonight in case she needs someone. Then in the morning I'll drive Martha into Wayford to the hospital."

"Mrs. Ryes, if you need anything tonight, please come and get me," the doctor offered. "My wife and I are in the last room on the second floor near the tall grandfather clock. Goodnight."

"Let's get you into bed," Helen said to Martha. "Chief Johns, will you please help me get Martha up the stairs and then I can do the rest?"

"Yes, of course. Come on Mrs. Littleword, let's get you into bed."

Martha flushed red. Helen's eyebrows knitted together, perplexed by Martha's reaction. She caught the quick, surreptitious glance Martha flashed at the Chief.

DCI Johns walked across the room and bent down, putting one arm under Martha's legs and one arm to support her back. He lifted Martha off the sofa and prepared to carry her up the stairs.

He moved so fast, she didn't realize it was happening until he was holding her up against his chest. Taken completely off her guard, Martha waved her hands in an effort to stop him from going anywhere.

"Oh, please. That isn't necessary. I can walk just fine," Martha said apologetically wiggling to free herself.

"Well, if you're sure." He put her back down on the couch. "I'll put my arm here for you to hold on to," he said offering his hand.

She took hold of his arm feeling the strength and solidness of his being.

As the three of them made their way upstairs, Martha found she kind of liked the way Johns smelled of pine and sandalwood. He was nice to lean on, too. His closeness was causing her head to pound again.

The Chief insisted on helping them to their room. Once in, they said goodnight and thanked him. As Martha shut door, she watched his figure move back down the darkly lit hallway.

"Nice."

"What?" Helen asked.

"Oh, nothing. Just enjoying the view."

70

SCENE BREAK

The girls went about their nighttime routines and Martha managed hers without any help. They turned out all the lights except the little lamp between their beds. Helen shoved a wingback chair under the door knob to the bedroom. She wasn't taking any chances.

Once they were finally tucked in under soft duvets and their eyes were shut, Martha said softly, "Someone pushed me, Helen. Down the stairs."

Helen sat bolt upright and looked at Martha who was still lying down, eyes shut and her hands loosely gripping the top edge of the duvet.

"Really?"

"Yep, really."

"Why didn't you say anything to the Chief Inspector?"

"I didn't want any more fuss made."

"Yeah, that's fine, but we're in a big house, in the dark, and a murderer is lurking about. Helen's voice rose with anxiety.

"I think it's the same person who shot Piers and whoever it is thinks I've seen something," Martha said with her eyes still shut.

Helen flopped back down on her pillows. She pulled the duvet up under her chin like a protective shield and closed her eyes. "Martha, we're in it deep."

"You said it, sister. Piers could be dying, I've got a psychotic killer hunting me, and don't you think Johns is attractive?"

Helen's eyelids flipped open. She turned her head to make sure it was Martha who was actually talking. "Are you kidding me? You put those three thoughts together in the same sentence?"

Then as an afterthought she mumbled, "Piers isn't going to die."

The room was quiet for a few minutes while Helen mused on what Martha had said. "You know, he is very strong and has a sense of power to his persona. Johns, I mean."

"I'll say, and I've got dibs on him. You and Piers would go nice together."

Then after a short silence, she continued, "Did you see Johns try and pick me up? He didn't even grunt or show signs of straining himself." The two women laughed out loud.

"Oh, Martha. You've got one of those womanly bodies. Men love that. As for Piers Cousins, he's too much to handle and I'm still burned from the whole George and Fiona situation."

They were both quiet again for a moment then Martha piped up.

"Helen, we're going to find out who is behind all this. For one, even though you won't admit it, you have your eye on Cousins so you probably don't want him dead. Secondly, I'm afraid for my life because some nut job thinks I know something or saw something. Maybe I have. I'm not sure what it might be though. And lastly, I'm bored."

"Bored? You're lying there with a concussion. These last two days have been more exciting than the last two decades of my life. If this is boring, I'd like to see your everyday life."

"Exactly. You're practically admitting how stale you life is. I want some excitement in my life, some adventure. What do you think? You in?"

Helen thought about it. Her job and her personal life was slowly grinding to a dull nub. She'd always loved a good mystery book. Why not live one instead?

"You know what? I'm in," she said decisively. "Besides, this situation has turned personal. Somebody tossed a corpse in my path and pushed my new best friend down the stairs. I owe them a payback."

"Aw, you're so sweet, Rambo," Martha cooed with her eyes still shut. "Let's get some sleep and come up with a plan tomorrow. Try to sleep with one ear open tonight. We've got to keep our wits about us from now on."

Less than five minutes later they were both completely asleep. A soft rain tapped outside on the window panes and the wind picked up, whispering and seeking entry amid the eaves of the old house.

Shadows played along the bedroom's walls and under the door. The doorknob twisted but entry was declined. A beautiful yet sturdy old wingback in a Colefax and Fowler chintz kept death at bay behind the door until it lost patience, and retreated to its own room for the night.

Chapter 17

"I'm glad you could come in this morning, Sir," Chief Johns said to Louis Devry on the following morning. "Have a seat." He motioned for Devry to sit opposite him on the other side of his desk.

"We haven't had this much violence in Yorkshire since Hindley and Brady wreaked their special brand of horror and murder in the 60's." Johns sipped his black tea out of a substantial yellow mug.

Louis Devry looked down at his hands, then turned them over and put his palms flat upon Johns' desk. "Chief Inspector, how can I help you? I apologize if I'm not myself. Piers Cousins is probably my best friend in the world and the nurse this morning said his condition is improving but he's weak."

Johns drummed his pen upon the desk. "You know, Devry, you've got an interesting accent. Can't place it. Where exactly are you from?"

"I was born in Hartford, Connecticut. My father was English and he taught anthropology at Harvard."

"How'd you end up in England?"

"We moved back to Oxford when I was twelve," Devry said.

"Is that where you met Piers Cousins?"

"I met Piers at Eton. On holidays I would go home with him to Healy. It was more of a home to me than my own. You see, my mother died when I was eleven and my father quickly remarried."

"So, you must have gone to Oxford or was it Cambridge?" Johns scribbled something in his notebook.

"Well, neither," Devry said with a short laugh. "I went to Harvard. I missed home."

"Did you work in America?"

"Yes. My first degree was in English literature so naturally one of the few avenues open to me was teaching. An absolutely exhausting experience. I taught in prep schools for a few years and then decided to go back and get my masters in curatorial studies. My first curatorial job was in Massachusetts working in a private collection."

Johns studied Louis Devry for a few seconds. "How did you end up here again, Mr. Devry?"

"About a year ago I got a phone call from Piers. He asked if I would be interested in a position with a museum he was involved with. I thought it would be a nice way to catch up with friends and I was aware of The Grange's famous collection. He invited me over for a look around and I wanted a change in my life, so I accepted."

"Do you have a wife, maybe a girlfriend?" Johns asked.

"Long time ago. The family I worked for after I finished my master's program had a daughter. Her name was Emilia. I fell in love with her but she was sent to school in Switzerland. I never married."

Johns pushed further. "What ever happened to Emilia?"

"She's dead." The muscle on the left hand side of Devry's jaw tightened and then relaxed.

Johns never took his gaze off Devry's face and was acutely aware of the man's every movement and energy. "How did she die?"

"In childbirth. It still happens you know? Women still die that way. She was extremely ill during the pregnancy and it took a toll. I was told something went wrong and she lost too much blood. She never regained consciousness. She died too young."

The last words were said more to the clenched hands in his lap than to Johns.

"What happened to the child? Did it live?" Johns asked.

Louis Devry actually blanched. Johns realized he'd hit a nerve.

75

"I…I…believe Emilia's husband, Sir Carstons, would have been raising the child."

There it was. An extremely bitter connection between the two men: a woman. Johns noted that Devry said "raising" not "father."

"Emilia was married to Sir Carstons?"

Devry nodded in the affirmative.

"He's been described as a brutal man. Do you know if he was the same with his wife and child?"

Devry took a deep breath and the vein in his neck pulsated visibly. "Emilia was a free spirit. I would like to believe she might have left Sir Carstons once the child was born. I'll never know, of course."

Johns decided to change direction in his questioning. "You said you'd gone to see your mother the day Sir Carstons was killed. A stepmother I presume?"

"Yes, Carissa is my stepmother but I call her mother. She's been like one to me since I was twelve. At first I resented her and made her life a hell, but she would bring me treats and knew how much I loved books. If there was ever a woman who truly loved me, it's Carissa. I've been blessed to have her in my life." He finished with a barely audible sigh.

"Mr. Devry where were you last night before Mr. Cousins was shot?"

Devry expression gave nothing away. "I'd gone up to my room. My head was killing me and I wanted to be done with the party. It was only when I heard the sirens coming up the road that I woke up."

"You'd fallen asleep?" Johns asked.

"I guess so because I remember coming to and hearing the noises outside. I got up and saw the ambulance and then the police out on the lawn. I went downstairs and ran into Mrs. Thyme. She was frantic and she told me what happened. I made a dash for the garden but they'd already put Piers on the gurney."

"You never heard the shot?"

"No. My windows were closed but my room is on the side of the house opposite the garden. I must have been sound asleep."

"I have one more question. Where did you go after you saw Cousins put into the ambulance?"

"I went back upstairs to my room. The whole evening, well in fact, the last three days have been a great strain."

Johns noticed the effort the man made during the interview to repress some type of intense emotion. "Mr. Devry, why have the last few days been particularly stressful for you?"

Devry took a deep breath and let it out.

"Carissa is fragile and there are extenuating circumstances that have nothing to do with all of this but they are weighing on my mind..." Devry's hands trembled.

He looked up at Johns and quickly asked, "Do you have a cigarette?"

"I don't smoke but my sergeant does. Hey Cross! Come in here a minute," Johns yelled.

The sergeant came into the room. "Yes, Sir?"

"Got a cigarette?" Johns asked.

"Sure do, Sir." Cross offered Johns his pack and Johns selected two from the middle.

"Thanks. That's all."

Johns offered Devry the cigarettes and handed him a lighter.

Devry lit a cigarette and inhaled the smoke. He looked directly at Johns and smiled. "Thank you."

"I think we're done here, but keep in mind, Mr. Devry, this is a murder investigation and in the event we need to get in touch with you, it's important you make yourself available. You do understand?"

"Of course. I'll leave my address. You have my number." Devry got up. "No more questions then, Chief?"

"No, not for now. I'll have Sergeant Cross take your statement. We'll also be taking a sample from your hands. Need to see if there's any gun powder residue on you."

Johns said this last part while studying Devry's face.

Devry didn't hesitate. "That's fine. Do what you need to."

He stubbed out his cigarette, thanked Johns, and followed Sergeant Cross down the hall.

Johns contemplated Devry's retreating figure. It was time to check out some background stories. Best to start with Devry's.

Chapter 18

Helen sat on a chair while Martha was comfortably propped up on a gurney in the middle of the radiology wing at the hospital in Wayford. Martha looked comfortable and content with herself. Since they'd arrived, she'd been charming people with her sweet smiles and referring to nurses as "Sweetie" and "Honey." Martha liked to spread it on thick especially when there was a possibility for needles or painful procedures in her immediate future.

Both she and Helen were feeling surprisingly energetic despite the exciting events of the previous evening.

"Mrs. Littleword are you ready to go into your screening?" a young nurse asked. Martha noticed that she looked younger than Martha's own daughter, Kate.

"I am, Honey," Martha said trying to exude cheerfulness.

"Martha, I'm going to check on Piers while you're in your screening. I'll be back here before you come out. Do you need anything?" Helen asked.

"No, you run along. I'll see you in a bit. Oh yeah, give him a hug for me," Martha said with a wink. "Might do you both some good."

"Oh good Lord." Helen laughed and rolled her eyes.

Scene Break

It took about ten minutes of wandering down hallways and following arrows to find the critical patients wing. A nurse stopped Helen to ask if she needed help.

"Yes, I'm looking for a gentleman brought in last night with a gunshot wound. His name is Piers Cousins. How is he doing today?"

"He's stabilized and in a room on the second floor. The nurses upstairs will be able to let you know if he's allowed visitors."

Helen took the elevator to the second floor and stopped at the nurses' station which was being manned by a bulky woman in her sixties. Her short, grey hairdo was reminiscent of the fight promoter, Don King's. She didn't look up when Helen asked if she might visit Cousins but instead put her pen down with exaggerated slowness. Her firm manner clearly conveyed to Helen that she was attempting to bridle her annoyance.

"I'll tell you what I've told the last three women who wanted to visit Mr. Cousins," she said with a tinge of menace. "He isn't ready for visitors but you can come back in the morning and get in line with the rest of his devotees if you wish."

Helen bridled at the inference. She read "Edda Davis" on the nurse's name tag. Firmly putting her purse down on the desk, she lowered her eyelids fixing her gaze on Ms. Edda's face.

"There is no reason to be snippy or insulting about my inquiry, Ms. Edda. I wanted to make sure he's out of critical condition," she said slowly back with one eyebrow arched.

The short nurse stood up and Helen realized it wasn't that she was short but that her chair was undersized. When the woman rose to her full height of around six feet, she was a formidable female. Helen, trying to stand her ground in the face of so formidable a force, swallowed with an effort to hiding her sudden intimidation.

"My break is in…," Ms. Edda said grimly looking down at her watch, "now. So, if you will excuse me." She turned her broad, muscular back on Helen and marched out of the nurses' area.

Helen exhaled air she didn't know she was holding and stood riveted to the spot watching Ms. Edda's departing backside move determinedly down the brightly lit hall. Relieved she hadn't been put to any tests of courage, she hesitated for a moment about what to do. Remembering how last night she'd decided to be more adventurous, she took stock of the situation and made up her mind. Quickly looking over the counter, she noted Piers' room number on the nurses' assignment sheet and then swiftly moved down the hall, a thrill of adventure filling her entire being.

Finding his room, she peeked inside. There he was, asleep in his bed with tubes and machines everywhere. For a moment, Helen wished she hadn't intruded but then his eyes opened and his gaze locked with hers.

"Helen?" he asked sleepily.

"Yes, Piers. I wanted to see how you were doing. I'm not supposed to be here."

"Come in," he said trying to sit up. "I won't rat you out to Ms. Davis."

Helen came in and sat down near his bed. "How are you feeling? Are you sure this won't tire you out?"

He readjusted himself and winced when he moved his upper body. "They patched me up. I was lucky because the bullet didn't hit anything too important. I'll have a great scar to impress the ladies with." He winked at her.

She laughed. "Honestly, Piers, I don't think you need one more thing in your repertoire to impress women."

"Depends on the woman. Some are impressed with wealth and others with power. What impresses you, Helen?"

"Integrity. Nothing sexier than integrity at this point in my life. But, you know, that's the hardest quality to find sometimes. It's not the mistakes that are made, it's the character a person shows when they're faced with their mistakes."

Piers studied her and smiled. "You're a straight shooter, Helen. That can be disconcerting and certainly not in my field of experience with most women."

"Piers," she said in a tone of complete honesty, "women, and men for that matter, sometimes let themselves be seduced by things that puff up their own egos. Like I said, you don't need one more thing to impress the ladies. All that probably gets in the way of knowing you."

She said all this in a gentle, friendly manner, but Helen decided to throw him a bone to make him feel better. She laughed. "Okay. You're handsome, rich, wonderfully well-mannered and now you'll have a great scar. You're a stud. Feel better?"

Piers' face broke out into a big smile and he chuckled. "Ouch! Oh, that hurts. What are you trying to do? Kill me?"

Helen's smile blazed momentarily then melted to a thin line. "No. I'm not, but someone most definitely tried to last night. At least they made it look that way."

"What an odd thing to say, Helen." Piers lay back on his pillow and shutting his eyes.

Helen admired the lines of his face. With his eyes shut, he was easier to look at directly. "You never know, Piers, maybe they wanted to get you out of the way."

"Well, I don't like their methods," he said wearily.

Helen was quiet for a moment. "Why didn't you like Sir Carstons?"

Piers' eyes opened and flashed briefly with a note of hostility before sadness crept into their corners. He turned his head to look out through the window into the sunny day beyond and said with vehemence, "Sir Alan Carstons was a vindictive, cruel man and he made innocent people pay for his insecurities and lack of a soul."

"Tell me how you really feel," Helen said, caustically trying to defuse his anger.

His face relaxed and he flashed those blue eyes at her again.

She quickly shifted tacks. "How did you ever get mixed up with him?"

He didn't immediately answer her, instead he pointed to the other side of the room.

"Helen, would you please bring me my wallet? It's over on the table."

She retrieved the wallet. Once he held it, he presented her with a picture of a small boy about six years old. The lad was golden-haired and holding a bubble-making pipe. There were bubbles in the air around his flung-back head and open, smiling mouth. One pudgy hand grabbed at the floating bubbles.

"A picture, they say, is worth a thousand words," he said.

She could imagine the sounds of a delighted child's laughter and knew in an instant that it must be Piers' child. "Yours?"

"Yes, and no," he said. "Suffice it to say, with Carstons' death, my life at The Grange is easier, but I am not so sure what this means for my suit to have custody of my son."

"Your son? How does Carstons fit into that picture?"

"Simply put, I had an affair with his beautiful and gentle wife, Emilia, and she became pregnant. I know the boy is mine but Carstons would never allow for a DNA test. I've been trying for years through every available legal channel to force his consent."

"What about the child's mother? Isn't the child with her?" Helen asked.

"His name is Emerson. No, she's dead. Emilia is dead. She died giving birth and I haven't been allowed to see the child."

Helen understood the full tragic force of the situation. What if the child was Piers'? What if Piers killed Carstons to expedite his suit to get the child? Helen knew nothing could stand between her and her children. Granted, they were all grown, but what a horrible situation for both of the men not to mention the child who was still so young.

"How did you get the picture?" she asked.

"I paid a detective to find the park where his nanny takes him to play. Then I sat down and waited every day for two weeks. I pretended to read a paper while he blew bubbles or tossed a ball only ten feet away. It was wonderful but also excruciatingly painful seeing him but not being able to be with him as his father. It made me even more determined to know him."

Then he added as if a second thought, "It was easy to get pictures."

"Did it make you want Carstons dead?" The words weren't supposed to be said out loud. She pulled back slightly cringing at her own words.

He didn't look up at her but continued to study the photo she'd handed back to him. "Yes, I hated him. He was in his own way a murderer because he drained the life out of tender things." He looked up at Helen. "I didn't kill him, though, and I wouldn't want his blood on my hands. Carstons was the kind of person who would be pleased if he was the reason you found yourself in hell."

Helen thought for a moment and then wanted to somehow make up for prying into his affairs. "Piers, I'm sorry. I'm being much to nosey."

He looked up at her with a warm, sincere smile. "I like talking this way. I like talking with you, Helen." Their eyes caught each others gaze. It was Helen who looked away first.

She spoke in a hurried manner trying to diffuse her sudden feeling of vulnerability, "I hope things work out for you with your custody suit. You've a lot on your plate. Martha and I need to go back to Healy to collect our things and wondered if we could pick up anything for you?"

He tried to sit up. "I would love my laptop. Also, would you please see if Mrs. Thyme could send me a care basket. She makes the best potato soup in the world. The food here is lacking in…" his comment trailed to a stop.

Helen thought to herself he was like a little boy who wanted a treat. It was impossible to resist. She patted his hand. "I'm on it, and by the way, when we go back to Healy I'm thinking about looking for the jerk who pushed Martha down the stairs."

"Do what?" Piers said sitting up again in his bed. He winced and held his side, asking in a croaking voice, "Martha was pushed down the stairs?"

"Go slow there, cowboy. Yeah, I should have dropped that bomb a bit easier, huh? After you were taken to the hospital, Martha went upstairs to get some aspirin. Someone came up from behind and pushed her. She's fine though. No stopping Martha." Helen smiled and shook her head.

Piers laughed. "Yes, Martha is not to be taken lightly. I wouldn't want to be on her bad side. There's a lot of heart there."

Helen cocked her head and gave him a thoughtful smile and a tender look. "Piers Cousins, you're a sweet man."

"You say that like you weren't sure before," he said with a short laugh.

"Be careful, Piers. Martha's on a mission and I've signed up, too. We're going to find the culprit who pushed her down the stairs. Who knows? Maybe we'll find your villain, too." She pointed to his bandaged wound.

She picked up her purse, told Piers to take a long nap, and then slipped out of the room.

The nurses' station was being manned by a male nurse chatting with a pretty nurse in pink scrubs. Ms. Edda wasn't back from her lunch, so Helen quickly walked in the direction of the stairwell door. Unnoticed and safe on its other side, she made her way down the stairs to find Martha and maybe some well-deserved lunch.

Chapter 19

"Do you think Piers might have killed Sir Carstons?"
Martha asked while she busily unwrapped a sandwich from
Harriet's Tea Shop.

"He certainly has a motive, don't you think? But he says he
didn't do it."

"Yeah. It's hard to imagine what it would have taken to
restrain myself from attacking Sir Carstons, if I'd been in Piers'
shoes," Martha said as she settled into her avocado and bacon
sandwich.

"I don't think he killed him though. I wouldn't be running
an errand for a killer."

Martha gave Helen a sideways look. "Oh, sure you
wouldn't."

Helen arched her eyebrows. "Martha, you don't know me
very well."

"Okay, sweetie. I was teasing you. I know you have
principles. But you have to admit that your gut feeling isn't much
to go on. Besides, suppose we found those security videos on his
computer before he got ahold of his laptop, then we would know
whether or not he knocked off Carstons."

Helen's reaction to this extremely brazen, if not unlawful,
suggestion was subdued. She was driving Martha's green Mini
Cooper while Martha ate her sandwich. Bringing the car to a
respectable, gentle stop, she turned and faced an oblivious,
munching Martha.

"Martha," Helen snapped. "Are you saying we should
snoop through Piers' laptop?"

Martha put the sandwich back down on her lap and picked
up the paper napkin. She dabbed daintily at the corners of her
mouth and swallowed. "I'm trying to dispel any worries you

might have about Piers by suggesting a possible way to find out if he's a killer or not."

Helen put the car back into gear and drove again. "Very thoughtful of you, Martha." Helen pursed her lips and then continued. "I think they call that obstructing justice and besides Piers had plenty of time to delete any videos of himself in the last day. Also, he could have turned off the cameras before attacking Carstons. But if you recall, he only remembered the security tapes after he was interviewed by the Chief Inspector."

"Maybe, but it might have been an act." Martha looked out into the grey day. "Okay, I guess we could always ask him if we can see them. If he gets touchy about it, then he's probably hiding something. What do you say?"

"I like it," Helen said as she pulled up in front of Healy House.

Getting out of the car and seeing the front door was open, they went inside. The house was quiet even though guests were still scattered about.

"An attempted killing hasn't run too many of them off," Martha said under her breath.

"The tournament is still going on so they probably have to stay."

Piers' study door was closed. The girls went inside and shut the door. On his desk still sat the laptop. Putting it into a satchel along with a power cord, they scanned the room but didn't see anything else Piers might need.

"Should we be taking this?" Helen asked. "I would have thought this room would be off limits. Wouldn't you?"

"No yellow 'do not cross' tape, so it must be fine."

The next item on their list was to find Mrs. Thyme. They asked a maid who directed them down a long hall leading to the kitchen.

As they approached, loud voices wafted up along the corridor. The girls plunged on and once within the kitchen's entryway, they saw Mrs. Thyme and what must be the head chef, a small, portly gentleman of Mediterranean heritage, embroiled in

87

a heated conversation. The chef's white uniform and apron were immaculate and he stood proudly like a statue upon a riser allowing him to work at one of the huge, steel tables.

"Chef Agosto, you must decide tonight's desserts," Mrs. Thyme said, stamping her foot. "I absolutely cannot put off knowing any longer. I have nine guests staying tonight and one couple is extremely fussy about the menu. It must be decided."

The little man stood firm. He looked down his proud, aquiline nose at her from his advantageous position on the riser and said with haughty dignity, "I will not be bullied, Madam. Not by you and certainly not by one of your fussy guests."

Then at the end of his speech, his voiced crescendoed giving the impression of a martyred culinary saint. "I decide the dessert when it is time and it is not the time!"

To put an absolute stop to any attempts at further discussion, he hopped down and hurriedly headed for the walk-in refrigerators. Stepping inside, he turned around, and glared at her like a small irascible badger.

"Senior. You are trying my last nerve. Come back here this minute!" Mrs. Thyme yelled after him.

"No!" he yelled back his chest expanding with his resolution. "You're a pushy woman and you're disturbing my thoughts. The whole meal is threatened by your aggressive behavior. Leave me, woman, while there is still time for me to regain my composure!" With a flourish, he pulled the refrigerator door closed with a slam, effectively ending the debate.

"I'm going to kill that mushroom of a man," Mrs. Thyme said under her breath. Then she yelled at the closed door, "Good! I hope you freeze in there! I'm not going to let you out, you short cretin from Spain!"

All they could hear in response was a muffled yell. "Leave-me-woman!"

Mrs. Thyme turned abruptly to see Helen and Martha staring at her with amused expressions. She pulled herself up into a more rigid version of herself and said in a highly annoyed manner, "The man is a swine. I'd like to toss him into the river out front but Piers loves him and thinks he walks on water."

She walked toward the girls. "You're here for the soup," she said, her temper waning.

"Yes, he wanted us to pick it up because we're heading back to The Grange and can drop it off on the way," Martha explained with a smile.

"I have it waiting up in my office." Mrs. Thyme walked with a deliberate stride back the way they'd come.

"What about Chef Agosto? Will he be okay in there?" Helen asked.

"Him? Oh, he will be just fine." She waved one arm in the direction of the kitchen. "He loves it in there because he can act like a mule and then stomp off into his refrigerator. Oh, don't worry, lasses, the door has a safety latch inside. Unfortunately."

Once in her office, Mrs. Thyme handed the girls a heavy plastic container full of potato soup. She pointed out the bag she'd packed for Piers.

"I've put in some nice toiletries and a few changes of clothes. His mobile is also in there. He's a sweet man, you know?" she said to both of them while never taking her eyes off the container of soup. "He doesn't have anyone to watch over him except me and I'm a poor excuse for a mother. He so loved Emilia and I didn't think he would ever get over her death. The child means everything to him but the situation worries me."

"What worries you about it Mrs. Thyme?" Martha asked.

She looked at the floor and then back at Martha. "I…I don't know if he's pushed it too far." Sinking down into her pillowed, wing-back chair, she continued in a tired voice. "So many horrible things have happened this last week. He's in danger, isn't he?"

"Mrs. Thyme, you're not to worry about Piers, okay? He's in safe hands at the hospital. But what do you mean, 'pushed it too far?'" Helen asked.

"He naturally wants his child. Any decent parent would. Do you think someone is trying to stop him from getting custody? I know Sir Carstons was such a brute and the child would inherit a fortune. Someone might want Piers dead so he isn't a threat with his suit anymore." She looked back and forth from Helen to Martha seeming to seek an answer from them.

"Mrs. Thyme, we think whoever murdered Carstons may have tried to kill Piers. His computer has surveillance videos which may show who the killer is," Martha explained. "Do you know of anyone at the party last night who is a good shot with a rifle?"

Mrs. Thyme considered Martha's sincere face. "The police asked that, too. So many of Piers' guests are regulars at his shooting parties in the fall. Practically everyone who was invited has been here before, so they would have a good idea of where the guns are kept, but they're always locked up. Louis Devry is an excellent shot. He and Piers used to go grouse hunting as boys here on the estate."

She sat quietly for a moment. The two younger women didn't ply her with anymore questions. Soon, she continued. "The police took most of the guns with them last night. Wait, here's something odd. This morning while I was looking for my cat out behind the kitchen garden, I saw where the vines were torn away from the wall. The wall is wide there. The gardener's son loves to walk on top of it, but he hasn't been home since the last school holiday."

"Do you mind if we take a look?" Helen asked.

"Sure, lasses. You run along. I've got lots of work to do and a Spanish mule to bring to harness." She lifted herself up from the comfortable old chair with a sigh. "Oh, by the way, please take this package to Piers. I found it this morning in the strangest place, the old linen cupboard in the cellar. I thought about putting it on his desk but with all the unusual happenings going on, I wasn't sure what to do with it. It might need to be at The Grange. He'll know what should be done."

She handed Martha a sizable manila envelope. Something clicked in Martha's mind. Hadn't she seen something like that before? But where?

Managing their parcels for Piers, they made their way out to the car.

"Let's put this in the Green Bean," Martha said referring to her Mini Cooper, "and then we can go check out the garden wall. Might be a clue."

The girls locked the car doors and went around the back of the house.

The kitchen garden connected to the enclosed garden where the party took place the night before, and both areas were situated behind Healy House. Along the face of the wall, many vines and flowering plants created comfortable homes giving the wall a feeling of a living thing. The girls could see where some of the vines were pulled away.

Sunning himself on the top of the wall was a black tabby Maine Coon cat. He lifted his head and yawned luxuriously.

"Must be Mrs. Thyme's cat," Helen said.

The cat opened his eyes widely and then went back to squinting in the bright sunlight. He rolled over and showed his soft, furry tummy as if trying to entice them into a nice scratch.

"Look at him, the scoundrel. I wonder if he'll actually let me pet him?" Helen moved toward the posing cat. She reached up as high as she could and gently scratched the top of his head between his two black ears. The cat purred loudly.

"He's a friendly old fellow," Martha said joining in the scratching but on the cat's tummy.

The cat, satisfied with their dutiful homage, rolled over on his side and put his back to them. Flicking his tail, he got up on all fours, did a deep back stretch, and sauntered off toward the top of the wall of the adjoining garden. He turned around, looked at them and artfully composed his tail in the shape of a shepherd's crook.

Martha and Helen took the bait and followed him along the wall until they came to the round opening in the stone work pointed out by the German guest the previous night.

"This is the spot where the gunshot may have come from," Martha said.

"Look. The police have put up their tape to keep everyone out. If someone wanted to shoot Piers, this would have been an excellent spot." Helen stuck her head and shoulders through the circle. "Hey. Look here, Martha. There's some kind of fabric hanging along the inside of the wall. I bet I can just reach it if I…"

Helen leaned in farther to grab the cloth. "Martha!" Screamed Helen as she lost her balance and fell forward head first through the hole.

Martha gawked as Helen's two feet flew straight up into the air. With a quick lunge at the up-ended legs, Martha grabbed the flailing ankles and pulled hard. She reached for Helen's belt and held it tightly until Helen could steady herself along the inside of the stone wall. Inching her hands upwards from stone to stone, Helen lifted herself until she reached the bottom ledge of the opening. Twisting herself around, she sat down inside the circular window for a minute and took a few deep breaths.

"Hey. You okay?" Martha asked, trying to catch her own breath.

Helen panted. "Whew. That's a steep drop on the other side. The ground is lower over there by probably two feet. Look what was hanging there. It looks like a torn piece of a dirty glove. You can see the shape of a finger section. The police probably wouldn't have been able to see it from their angle last night."

"Let's keep it and show it to Chief Johns when we get back to the village. Might be a good clue." Martha's tone was that of delight. Actually finding something the police had missed might be a nice way of seeing Johns again.

"Why would anyone scramble along the edge of the garden wall then drop down and shoot someone from this opening? All they would have to do is walk around. Right?" Martha pointed out.

"True. Why indeed?" Helen dropped back down to the ground to stand by Martha.

They stared up at the wall and the circular opening. Then both turned slowly around to view the fields stretching out behind the gardens. The answer hit them both at the same time. The field was actually an enclosed area. Down near the opposite edge of the field, they could see small wooden buildings resembling kennels.

"Dogs. Of course," Helen said still studying the grounds below them.

As if on cue, three German Shepherds rounded the corner of the far edge of the kitchen garden and charged toward Helen and Martha.

"Oh, my God! Let's get out of here!" Martha screamed.

"Where?" Helen yelled back, her whole body rigid.

"The wall!"

Without a second of hesitation, Helen jumped back into the round opening she'd only just left minutes ago and used it as a step to scramble onto the stone wall above them. Martha followed her and in short measure both women were working their way along the top of the wall while the three massive dogs growled and bounded beneath them.

"Why don't they bark?" Martha yelled at Helen.

"How should I know?" Helen yelled back. "Maybe they're trained to stalk their quarry quietly and then rip out their throats."

"Lovely visualization, Helen," Martha said, trying to keep her balance on the wall.

"Seems like a practical interpretation."

They reached the kitchen section of the gardens and found the cat squinting at them from the safety of the roof.

Martha glowered at the cat. "I think that rascal knew exactly where he was taking us."

They found a ladder leaning against the inside of the wall and made their way down into the safety of the kitchen garden.

"No, Martha. I think the cat was showing us a clue and how the person must have managed to circumvent the dogs last night," Helen said.

She gave a short salute to the cat who responded with an indifferent yawn before flopping onto his side with his back to them. Ignoring them completely, he began his daily ablutions focusing on his right hind leg.

"You never know who to thank in this business, do you?" Martha laughed, looking at the cat's backside.

"Come on. Let's get out of here," Helen said. "All this excitement is making me hungry. That sandwich didn't fill me up."

Martha, delighted with the idea of eating again, added, "Danger makes me hungry. I know the place. The cook is partial to comfort food. Sound good?"

Helen nodded. "Let's do it. We better eat quickly. Louis Devry is meeting you at The Grange at three. Don't want to keep the boss waiting."

Chapter 20

The Traveller's Inn was always a busy hostelry in Marsden-Lacey on a Sunday afternoon. Church was over and so was Sunday dinner. The local villagers who were interested in football liked to congregate at The Traveller's to watch the game, drink a few pints and yell at the television. Of course, it was also a great place to enjoy a good meal and to slip away from one's nearest and dearest.

DCI Johns walked with determination down the High Street to The Traveller's intending to have a bottle of Fullers porter and a nice plate of pie and mash. He sensed something in his comfortable and established reality was shifting and he needed a nurturing environment and a good meal to settle his thoughts. This slight shift in what he'd always known, had come out of the blue and, more irritatingly, without his consent. As he pushed the old, iron-studded door to the pub with a heave, his gaze rested on Lilly, the barmaid, serving Doc Whithersby at the bar.

Johns plumbed the depths of that deviation again as he looked for a place to sit near Lilly and found something missing there and not likely to realign itself anytime soon. He no sooner averted his eyes from Lilly and Whithersby's cozy tête-à-tête, when his gaze fell on the tasseled mane of a red-haired woman.

His heart took a leap and banged against the fault line which he was now certain had moved irrevocably. Quickly doing an about face and heading for the opposite side of the pub, he joined the old men who liked to sit by the fire and talk about how the government was testing their faith in the future of England. Johns sat down with a huff and glared at the back of that fluffy, red pile of hair.

What in the world had gotten into him? Lilly was the type of woman he'd always imagined for himself. She was slim, dark-haired with almond-shaped eyes and a serenity he admired. From his old-man corner, he watched Whithersby flirt with Lilly while she laughed at the doctor's probably feeble attempts at humor.

Johns shifted his glance again to look at the mess of red hair bobbing about with every move of the woman's head. He wondered at its curls and the way it glowed from the soft sunbeams streaming through the windows. Probably smelled good, too, he thought.

The head turned around and he stiffened. He immediately focused intently on his beer bottle. Without looking up, he heard the two women chatting and getting nearer to his table. Raising his gaze from his bottle, he gave the two arrivals at his table a slim smile.

"DCI Johns. What a nice surprise to find you here. We might have a clue to share with you," Helen said, practically bubbling with good humor.

Martha stood behind her, looking through her purse.

"A clue? What have you two been up to?" Johns tried to mimic Helen's pleasant tone.

Martha looked up and squinted in the dusky light at Johns.

"We were at Healy picking up some things for Piers and decided to look around near the spot where we thought the shooter might have been hiding," Helen said. "We found a torn piece of a glove." She took the plastic bag Martha finally retrieved from her purse and handed it to Johns.

"Ladies," he said in a low, gravelly voice, "you didn't cross the pretty yellow tape we wrapped around the entire garden, did you?" And then, in a 'how I talk to idiots' tone, he added, "There is an attempted murder investigation going on and tampering with the site will get you arrested."

Both Helen and Martha, seemingly indifferent to his barbed sarcasm, pulled out chairs and sat down. There apparent chumminess took Johns by surprise and his gaze darted back and forth between the two of them.

"We think," Helen said, "the video files hold the answer to who killed Sir Carstons. We would like to see them."

"What? You? Absolutely not!" Johns pulled himself upright and looked at them like they were crazy. "What on God's green Earth makes you think I'm in the habit of sharing evidence or teaming up with…with…the general public on an investigation?"

"Why not?" Martha reached over and took a swig out of his beer bottle.

Grabbing the bottle back from her with another shocked look, he said, "Because the police are not in the habit of confiding and sharing evidence with the public. That's why."

Martha leaned back in her chair with a twinkle in her eye and crossed her arms. "You don't have the files, do you? In fact, I bet you're having to wait until Piers is deemed okay by his doctor before he can be interviewed and you can check out those files."

Johns found himself suddenly attuned to Martha's closeness and at the same time thrilled with her nerve. How dare she taunt him with the truth about how he didn't have the files yet? How dare she try and steal his beer? Was the woman baiting him or was she simply crazy?

"Mrs. Littleword and Mrs. Reyes, if I find out you are in any way messing about in either of my investigations, I will lock you up. Do you understand?" He tried to sound in command.

Helen, sitting in her usual straight-back, debutante manner, gave Johns a look that would have wilted a weaker man. She remained silent.

Martha responded. "We're only trying to help because we feel personally involved in both incidents. If you wish to throw us in jail, then you had better get on with it because we have no intention of ignoring our duty to our friends or this community."

Martha rose from her chair in a regal hauteur. "Come, Helen. We're not getting anywhere with the Chief. We were trying to be helpful and he doesn't appreciate our efforts. We've got places to be."

The girls exited The Traveller's Inn, leaving Johns to ponder his newly-arrived plate of pie and mash. He wasn't sure whether to arrest them or to eat his dinner. The food won out.

While he ate, his mood lifted and he found himself secretly pleased with the notion of himself as a commandant. He studied the fabric through the plastic bag. Better give it to forensics.

His mind went back to the shocking moment when Martha actually took a drink out of his beer bottle. The act was brash and audacious yet somehow enticing. He smiled to himself and finished the beer.

There was definitely something about that woman he was finding hard to ignore.

SCENE BREAK

The Mini Cooper hummed along the main road leading to Wayford. Louis Devry had not made his interview appointment with Martha again so the girls decided to drive to the hospital to drop off Piers' things. With the car's top down and the rolling English pastures in lush summer finery, they couldn't help admiring the views in the hazy, soft evening light.

Helen drove while Martha fiddled with the radio. Finding a station playing old tunes from the Rat Pack's heyday, the girls sang "Fly Me To The Moon" along with Old Blue Eyes. They enjoyed reliving their adventure atop the old garden wall and laughed at their conversation with Johns in The Traveller's. Neither had felt so alive in years.

Ten minutes later they pulled into a visitor parking place at the hospital in Wayford. Piers was being allowed visitors so there was no need to sneak past the nurse's station. According to the nurse who was busily doing paperwork, Piers was with a visitor and they would have to wait their turn.

Soon, a tall, slim woman came sashaying down the corridor. Lana Chason stopped mid-stride. Recognizing Helen and Martha, her face brightened and she quickened her step toward them.

Martha and Helen offered her weak grins of acknowledgment and waited to see where it would go from there.

"I'm so glad to see a pair of friendly faces. There's a nurse here who frightens me," Lana said looking over her shoulder nervously. "Are you here to see Piers, too?"

Martha, clutching the huge bag packed by Mrs. Thyme, gave one of her cheery smiles. "Yes, we've been given the job of delivering Mrs. Thyme's soup."

"Oh, he'll be much happier to see you then. I'll warn you, he's in a grumpy mood." Lana pouted. "Actually, I'll be completely honest. He's like a caged lion in there and I wouldn't be surprised if he tries to make a break for it." She shrugged and settled one perfectly-manicured hand on her hip. "He's crazy if he tries. That nurse I mentioned is like one of my brother's old bloodhounds. She's got his scent and there'll be no slipping away for him anytime soon. You girls be careful. I'm heading home tonight. When you see him, open the conversation with the soup."

Martha and Helen waved goodbye and watched Lana float like a warm Louisiana breeze down the corridor and through the main doors.

"She's definitely got charm," Helen said smiling as the hospital doors slid shut.

"You know, I love that southern accent. It's delicious," Martha said thoughtfully. "Hmm…Are you hungry?"

"Oh for Pete's sake, Martha. We just ate. Twice. Come on. Let's go see Piers. We're going to have to go to the museum again. I left my briefcase. I don't know where my head is these days." The girls stood up and walked down the hallway to Piers' room.

"Let me get the soup out before we knock on the door. We need to butter him up a little if we want to get a look at those videos." Martha riffled through the substantial bag. "Helen, wasn't there a package or something Mrs. Thyme gave us to give to Piers? It's gone. Maybe it fell into the floorboard of the car. I hope it's there."

The girls found the door to Piers' room and began to knock but hesitated when they heard two men talking within. Martha held her finger up to her lips in a hush signal and both women listened in on the conversation.

Piers was talking. "I'm waiting for the laptop. Helen and Martha are supposed to be dropping it by soon. No one has the password but me, so I doubt if there's any way the video files could have been tampered with. Besides, why do you want to see them? Please tell me, Louis, you didn't off Carstons."

Martha and Helen raised their eyebrows at each other but kept their ears close to the door.

"Piers," Louis Devry said in a nervous voice, "of course I didn't kill him but those videos are going to be requested by the police and there may be something in them I...well you see... Okay, Piers, I need to be frank with you about something delicate."

"What are you two doing out here with your ears pressed against the door?" came a strong and commanding voice from behind Martha and Helen.

They jumped and went stiff. Slowly turning around, they raised their gaze upward to find themselves staring slack-jawed into the pugnacious, stern face of Nurse Edda Davis.

Chapter 21

Martha, feeling small, stuttered, "We were waiting to see when it was okay to go in for a visit."

Nurse Davis' expression implied she wasn't buying what Martha was selling. She compressed her lips in distaste and pointed repeatedly with a jabbing motion at where they'd been sitting. "Ladies, visiting hours are over in ten minutes. You may wait out by the nurses' station."

Since she wasn't moving, they meekly backed away and found their way back to the row of seats they'd left moments earlier. The girls sat down like chided children.

Martha was the first to speak. "We aren't going to have a chance to talk with Piers."

Staring at the door, Helen said, "We may need to hide somewhere until she's gone. Visiting hours are almost over and, if we're going to talk with Piers before tomorrow, we've got to find a way around Edda the Hun."

"Was that Devry's voice we heard?" Martha asked.

"Sure sounded like it." Helen was quiet for a second. "What might be on those videos Devry doesn't want anyone to see?"

"Maybe he's the killer but he's lying about it and he's trying to make a deal with Piers. We need to get to Piers before tomorrow. He might be less willing to discuss things, if he has time to think about it or if Chief Johns gets the video footage first."

They watched the clock above the nurses' station closing in on the six o'clock hour. The best plan they'd hatched involved slipping into the ladies room near the stairwell and waiting until the coast was clear. Then, they could make their way into Piers' room.

At ten after six, Louis Devry walked down the hall toward them. He stopped and said hello but excused himself before they could ask why he missed his appointment with Martha.

"He was in a snit," Martha said as she clutched her bag in a readying position for their running of the hospital gauntlet.

"We're hopefully about to find out," Helen said rising. "Follow me."

The girls hurriedly moved in the direction of the room. Not seeing Nurse Edda patrolling the hall anywhere, they found Piers' door open. With great caution, they peeked in to make sure he was alone. There stood Nurse Edda settling a tray on the moveable bed table. With every effort to stay invisible, they backed away quietly and made a beeline to the ladies room letting the door close shut on its own volition.

"Okay, let's give it ten minutes and peek out. If it's clear, we go straight to his room. We'll have to be quick and quiet. God knows where that woman will be," Helen said.

"Our luck she'll need to use the rest room," Martha said sourly.

Helen and Martha froze.

"Really?" Helen asked.

As if on cue, they heard someone coming toward the door talking loudly. The girls frantically jumped into one stall and shut the door. Fortunately, the hospital was an old one from the early twentieth century and not many updates had been made to the bathrooms. The particular stall they bustled into was more like a small closet but someone looking from the outside could see an individual's feet, if they bent down to check if the stall was occupied.

"Get up on the back of the toilet," Helen hissed in a low frantic voice. "Hurry."

Martha scrambled up as high as she could while Helen climbed up on the toilet seat. Trying not to breathe too loudly, they were as quiet as possible.

The main bathroom door swung open and someone clattered around trying different stalls. Hurriedly, Helen pressed her foot against the stall door to make sure it wouldn't budge. It was perfect timing because a second later the person pushed on their stall door.

"These stupid stall doors," the voice of Nurse Davis grouched. "Everything in this hospital is falling apart." Going down the line she entered another stall and the door latch clicked.

Helen motioned for Martha to follow her. She gingerly opened the stall door and they crept out of the bathroom with only a small creak from the door's hinges to hint at their escape. As quick as mice, they scuttled into Piers' room to find him glowering at a plate full of nasty-looking noodles.

"Hey. What are you two doing here?" he asked brightly with a big smile spreading across his face. "You look like you're on the run from the law. I'll get dressed and you can break me out of this place. What do you say?"

Martha and Helen dropped into the two chairs across from his bed and let out two big breaths of air.

"We've been playing a game of cat and mouse with your Ms. Edda." Martha fumed. "DCI Johns ought to give her a job at the Marsden-Lacey Constabulary. She'd make an incredible detective."

"Not to mention a deterrent to crime." Helen weighed in with a laugh.

"Doesn't seem to have deterred either of you," Piers said with a knowing smile. "It's way past visiting hours so both of you are in it deep, if she catches you."

"With that in mind, let's get down to business then," Martha said. "We brought your soup and we brought your laptop. What say you start sipping on the one and let us have a look at the other?"

"Martha," Helen said with a hint of incredulity. "What about being subtle?"

"We don't have time for subtleties, Helen. Attila could come in any minute. Piers, the videos may show who knocked-off Sir Carstons. The police want the videos and it sounded like Devry has an interest in them as well. We think you ought to look at them and see who might have tried to take a potshot at you. Whoever it is has decided Helen and I are dispensable too. What do you say?"

"Give me the laptop," Piers commanded, laying down his spoon and a cracker.

They watched him open the security program and log in. He found the file for the day of the murder.

"The great thing about this system is the surveillance is always kept in the cloud. Only someone who has the password to my cloud can access the videos. I've not shared my password, so all should be as it was," Piers explained.

He clicked on the file for last Friday, the day of Carstons' murder. They watched the video load. Piers sipped on his soup. "I love Mrs. Thyme's soup. The food here is horrific."

"Spoiled baby," Helen teased softly.

"Look. If you put the video on slow fast-forward we can see people coming and going all morning. The time is in the right-hand corner." Martha reached over to click on the arrows in the video program's screen.

As the video played, they saw Sir Carstons enter The Grange. He circumvented the reception desk and looked around furtively. Unhooking the red rope blocking the way up the grand staircase, he quickly ascended the stairs and out of camera view.

"What is our friend, Carstons, up to?" Piers asked sardonically. "We'll change cameras and see where he's going."

Piers opened another file from a camera labeled "Upstairs Hallway." Sir Carstons appeared, walking down the hall and into one of the rooms to the right. A shadow moved across the floor and a figure came out from another side room.

"It's Louis Devry. He's following Carstons," Helen said.

All three peered intently at the video. Soon Carstons came out of the room carrying a satchel and headed back in the direction of the stairs followed by Devry. They both appeared to be agitated and in a hurry.

Piers switched the camera back to the "Reception Room." There it picked up Carstons coming down the stairs. He was carrying the satchel and Devry bounded down the stairs behind him apparently shouting at him. Carstons held up the bag, taunting Devry who made a quick move, whisking it out of Carstons' grasp, then leaping behind the reception desk.

Surprised, Carstons leaned over the reception desk and tried to grab the satchel while Devry leaned as far back as he could to avoid his grasp.

"Wow. They're going at it," Martha said with a chuckle.

Devry clutched the bag to his chest and pointed his finger at Carstons, yelling something and pointing to the door. He reached into the satchel, dragged out an oversized orange envelope, and then threw the empty bag at Carstons.

Carstons picked it up the satchel and made a stabbing motion with his index finger while obviously yelling something at Devry. He turned and stalked out The Grange's front door. The clock on the video said "14:30 Friday." Devry walked out of the room to the right in the direction of the library.

"This seems to be in keeping with what Louis was telling me," Piers said. "Sir Carstons was blackmailing Louis. He knew that Louis lost his job at Harvard for some indiscretion and offered to keep his mouth shut if Louis would turn a blind eye to Carstons helping himself to a few items of value at The Grange. According to Louis, Carstons showed up that day to make good his demand. Louis says he found him in one of the rooms going through some of the poetry books and hand-bound journals worth an enormous amount of money to crooked collectors. It was money Carstons sorely needed for legal fees." Piers glanced at Helen.

"What's in the envelope he took out of the satchel? Is it the poetry books and the journals?" Martha asked. She'd recognized the manila envelope and wondered if it could possibly be the one Mrs. Thyme found and gave them earlier that day.

"Louis says he took it back to his office. He wanted Helen to check it out to make sure it wasn't damaged in any way."

"Oh," Martha said, but something didn't fit. She shifted topics. "Carstons left The Grange alive though. I should be arriving in about thirty minutes and Devry must have been in his office."

They fast forwarded the video until they saw Martha walk through the door, peek over the counter then wander down the hallway in the same direction Devry had earlier. The time counter showed the minutes ticking by and then they saw Carstons sneak back into the hall. He moved around the reception desk. The video jumped and then only the reception area was visible. Sir Carstons disappeared into thin air.

"That's odd," Helen said. "Where did Carstons go? Wait. Look. There's Martha and me coming into the reception area."

From that point on in the video, everything happened as expected. Though they replayed the video multiple times, the same section of the video showing who killed Carstons was gone. It had clearly been removed.

"Someone knows your password, Piers, and they've altered the video. Almost everyone in the house the night of the party had access to your laptop," Martha said. "Do you keep a copy of your passwords anywhere?"

"Not where they're easily found. Someone might have seen where I hide my password book. I'm not sure."

"Of course," Helen said. "Whoever was in your office the night of the party was probably trying to get to the videos. That's why Martha was pushed down the stairs because they think she knows or might have an idea who they are. I think it's Louis Devry. He had every opportunity and he must have been desperate to get those videos. I think he's our killer and the person who shot you, Piers."

There was a stunned silence in the room once she finished. Helen shifted her gaze from Piers' face to Martha's.

Piers pushed away the laptop and sighed. "Louis already came here this evening and explained himself. Yes, he was aware of the video surveillance system after the fact, but he wouldn't have any way to know my password or where to find my password book. As for shooting me, I don't know. He's a good shot but he would have to be an incredible shot. Whoever shot me somehow missed Lana. The bullet went right over her shoulder and entered here, basically missing every major organ." He pointed to the area around his clavicle.

"Piers, someone was desperate to get you out of the way to save their own skin. You said it yourself that night. Helen and I heard you as you came out of your office saying the surveillance system had been installed and no one but you would have known of its existence. The killer had to have either overheard your conversation or been a part of it. Since I find it unlikely that DCI Johns is our murderer, that only leaves Devry," Martha argued.

"Hold on Martha," Helen joined in, "anyone might have been listening as they came out of the library and learned of the cameras being installed. The house was full of people. We heard him talking so others could have, too."

"No one else has a motive, Helen, well at least not one we're privy to."

"The question is who would have been able to learn of your password, be adept at accessing the video software and then editing the video? Are there back-ups of the video, Piers, stored somewhere?"

"I'm cursing myself because I didn't invest in the surveillance system sooner."

Female laughter from outside the door made Piers, Martha and Helen go rigid. Helen jumped into the lavatory while Martha made a quick dash for the wardrobe. They'd barely sequestered themselves, when a young nurses' voice could be heard asking, "All done with your meal Mr. Cousins?"

"Yes, thank you," Piers replied.

"Where did you get the soup?"

"My friend brought it to me from home."

"Best not let Ms. Davis know about it. She doesn't like people bringing patients food from the outside."

"I promise not to tell, if you don't," Piers said, his voice charming.

There was a rattling of dishes and they heard the door swing open.

"You're safe with me, Mr. Cousins. Get some rest. It's almost lights out and Ms. Davis will be down to give you your bath and tuck you in. Good night."

The door closed and out popped the girls from their hiding spots.

"Okay. We've got to dash, Piers," Helen said in a hurried voice. "The police will be by tomorrow to see those videos. Might not mention that Martha and I have already had a look. In the meantime, we're going to The Grange to check on some things. Whoever might have guessed at your password is extremely dangerous."

"That's right. You've got to be careful. They've tried to cover their steps by editing the videos but they don't know if there's a back-up, which makes things dicey." Martha said. "Did you tell Devry there wasn't a back-up?"

"No. He didn't even ask. That means he has to be innocent, right?"

"Not exactly. It may simply mean he isn't showing his concern which might make him look guilty. All it takes is a phone call to the software company you bought the system from, to find out about the options you purchased," Martha said.

"We've got to get out of here. Piers, we'll call later. Keep your cell phone close. If you think of anything, call us," Helen said.

The girls waved good-bye and peeked out the door. Two nurses sat in their station while a custodial person waxed floors with a loud machine. The noise was a great cover for slipping down the hallway unnoticed.

"No time like the present," Martha said and off they went.

Half-way past the station, one tired nurse looked up and gave them a quizzical glance but simply shrugged and went back to her reports. They whipped through the reception area. When they were within yards of the exit, an alarm blared above their heads.

Hospital personnel raced toward Martha and Helen. The girls froze. They stared with horrified faces at their pursuers, feeling like guilty criminals. However, the hospital staff completely ignored them as the sliding doors of the entrance flew open and an emergency team yelled at them to stand back. Martha and Helen jumped to the side and watched the EMTs rush past pushing a gurney with a man on it.

The commotion swirled around the girls and then moved rapidly away down the corridor. Helen and Martha stood gawking after the moving maelstrom.

"Let's get out of here." Martha said heading to the exit.

Helen followed on her heels. "I'm right behind you."

Chapter 22

Wayford and Marsden-Lacey were only fifteen minutes apart. The day had been extremely long and both Helen and Martha were ready for a glass of wine, soft beds and sweet dreams. However, they had one last errand to run.

As they drove along the quiet English countryside, the evening air was tinged with a coolness that helped to clear their brains of any dullness or fatigue. Crickets and frogs sang soft lullabies in the hedgerow while moonlight gave the rounded haystacks, still drying in the fields, a ghostly luminescence. The Mini Cooper meandered along the peaceful country road bordered by ancient stone walls, with the occasional pretty cottage tucked into a grove of trees. It was a busy, nighttime Marsden-Lacey they drove through with tourists and locals alike out taking strolls, window shopping and enjoying the summer evening air.

Pulling into the parking area to the west of The Grange, Helen turned off the car's motor and headlamps. She slumped a bit, leaned over and hugged the steering wheel, resting her chin on its top curve. The Grange was a world apart from the village below. No one was about and only one meager security lamp was trying its best to light the area. Without the drone of the car's engine, the growing darkness and the deep silence of the night settled on the girls with a heaviness similar to the air right before a thunderstorm. The silhouette of the old Elizabethan building, backlit by a bright crescent moon hanging above its chimneys rose up in front of their car. For a moment both girls were aware of their hesitation to get out and enter the dark, empty building.

"You know what?" Helen asked softly while studying the scene through the windshield.

"What?" Martha murmured in response.

"I don't want to go in. This whole situation seems to be getting very edgy."

"No kidding. I'm wishing I had a big stick," Martha replied. "Fortunately, I know how to use my hands as lethal weapons."

Helen gave Martha's hands a cursory glance but didn't seem impressed. "Yeah, right. We probably ought to go get Chief Johns before we start looking around."

"Nah, my instincts say it'll be okay. Remind me again of why we're going in there?" Martha asked shooting a nervous glance over at Helen.

"I need to get my briefcase. I've got my calendar and my phone charger in it."

"Somewhere in this car I have a flashlight." Martha dug around in the car's floorboard under her feet. Something was lodged halfway under the seat but it didn't feel like a flashlight. Reaching down, she pulled a bulky package out of its tight spot.

"Hey. Look what I found." She held up a good-sized, yellow envelope.

"Where was it?" Helen asked.

"It must have fallen out of the bag Mrs. Thyme gave us and my foot pushed it back under the seat." Martha smiled knowingly at Helen and arched one eyebrow. "What does this remind you of?"

In less than a second, Helen remembered. "The envelope in the video. It looks like the one Louis Devry took out of the satchel. This must be the book of poetry Sir Carstons was trying to steal. What a relief to know its safe."

"Yeah, but it's not waiting for you at The Grange, is it? It's been hidden for some reason in a linen closet at Healy." Martha plopped the envelope down on her lap and squeezed the metal bracket which kept the envelope closed.

She pulled out the contents. It appeared to be many pages of paper bound together. The writing was in someone's natural hand but in a more florid, antique style. Helen's curatorial instincts were flashing red. She always got a funny feeling when she was near something exceptional.

111

"Turn the overhead light on. May I look at it?" Helen asked.

Martha shrugged and relinquished the manuscript over to Helen who took it and began riffling around in her purse pulling out some small eyeglasses. Putting them on, she studied the front cover of the carefully hand-bound manuscript.

"Martha, this isn't a book of poetry. In fact it isn't a published volume at all. It's a handwritten manuscript. I won't take it out of the mylar bag until I have the right equipment and gloves. Something isn't right about this. Let's go get my briefcase and a few other things I need to examine this more closely."

"Okay, we should hide it again don't you think? Under the seat would be good. I'll take my flashlight with us." Martha started a fresh search of the car finally digging in the glovebox and unearthing a small silver flashlight.

They gently put the manuscript back into the envelope and tenderly maneuvered it under the passenger seat. Martha put a few things around it to hide it from view. Once out of the car, they locked the doors and walked in the dark with the flashlight to the side entrance.

The garden walkway was easy to traverse. Moonlight illuminated the white gravel path allowing the girls to confidently find their way to the door the staff used to access the building. A thoroughly modern metal door, half-hidden by two flanking cypress shrubs, told Helen she'd found the right place. With a wave of her badge across the security pad, a red light began to flash followed by a solid green light. The door made a click sound and Helen gave it a firm push to open it.

Once both women were inside with the door shut, they found themselves in a dark hallway lit by a security light giving off a red glow. Helen felt for the light switch and flipped it on eliciting a sigh of relief from both women once the hall was ablaze with comforting, familiar florescent light.

"Glad you found it," Martha said. "The red light was definitely not giving me a warm, fuzzy feeling."

"Follow me. I want to see if there are any other manila envelopes on Devry's desk."

"Good idea. I'm right behind you."

As they rounded the corner, Helen spotted one of the new camera's monitoring the hallway Devry's office was located in.

"We can't go in, Martha. Look."

"Keep walking until we're past it. Then give me a minute."

Martha and Helen strode down the hall and walked under the camera.

"Got any gum or something sticky in your purse?" Martha asked while digging in her own.

"Here's some gummy worms," Helen said pulling a small bag of candy from her jacket pocket.

Martha looked surprised. "I'd never figured you to be a gummy kind of girl."

"I like the sour ones best."

Helen handed Martha two worms who mushed them together into a ball.

"I'm going to lift you up, Helen, and your going to mash this gummy stuff into the lens of the camera. Got it?"

"Okay, let's go."

Making a stirrup of her hands, Martha gave Helen a leg up to reach the camera. Easily, the gummy goo was puttied over the lens and Helen was back on her own two feet within a few seconds. They could now get on with their earlier intention.

Devry's office door was locked. Undeterred, Martha took out a metal nail file with a notch on its end and fiddled with the old door's lock until it turned.

"It's open," she said softly.

Helen reached into the room and flipped on the light. From the doorway they could see how tidy he kept his office but not one manila envelope could be seen anywhere.

"Hmm? What do you think, Helen? Should we maybe poke around a bit? Lift papers up and look under them?" Martha flipped a pile of papers on Devry's desk so she could see what was under them.

"Maybe we could also open a desk drawer or a file cabinet," Helen replied.

With nothing to hold them back, they perused the room with an efficiency the CIA would have found admirable but not a single manila envelope turned up.

Martha stood up from where she'd been digging through Devy's lower desk drawers. "I think it's conclusive. Not one single book of poetry in here."

"Or it wasn't ever a poetry book in the first place. Maybe it's what's inside the manila envelope in your car. Come on let's get my stuff and go to your house," Helen said. "I want to get a better look at that manuscript. My briefcase is in the library. Follow me."

Tidying up after themselves in Devry's office and re-locking the door, they made their way to the library. Helen found her briefcase and her laptop, and checked to make sure she had cotton gloves and her phone charger.

"Everything I need is here. We should be able to get some information about the manuscript tonight," Helen said while packing up her things.

"My question is why was it found in a linen cupboard at Healy? Odd, don't you think?"

"Someone was hiding it, I guess. It's as if they were in a hurry. Who knows though? It could be something someone laid there years ago."

"Gotcha there, my dear. The envelope wasn't made in the UK. It had a 'Made in Exton, PA' along the fold and it had a bubble wrap liner. Couldn't be too old," Martha noted.

"You're good." Helen was delighted with Martha's observational powers. "We would make a great detective team."

Without warning, the lights in the library went out. Martha and Helen could feel their hearts leap into their throats. The meager light filtering into the huge room came from the signs designating the exits.

"Get under the table," Helen commanded.

The old library table was made of oak. If someone wanted to do a jig on it, it wouldn't make a creak. Along one side of its length were short shelves full of books and along its short length was a desk which Helen used for her work. As they quickly hid themselves under the table, the door to the library slowly opened. A flashlight beam scanned the room.

The girls dared not breathe. From their position under the table, they watched the beam of light flip around then stop right above their heads on the tabletop. Light footsteps approached the desk but due to the darkness, it was impossible to see who the intruder was.

Instinctually, the idea of this being more foe than friend began to creep upon them. The feeling they were being stalked was palpable. Martha and Helen could hear the blood banging in their ears.

Footsteps stopped and an unnatural voice pierced the darkness, sounding metallic, crazed and false. "Come out, come out wherever you are. You can't run and you can't hide. You'll never leave this place alive."

Martha flinched and Helen wrapped herself around her briefcase.

Palatable fear made Martha act. With all her might she pushed one of the larger bookshelves positioned up against the library table. The community of shelves were linked together. If one went over, they all went. Shelves crashed one after the other against the wooden floor, making a noise so tremendous it could have awakened the dead.

Martha, forgetting her flashlight, scrambled out from under the desk with Helen in tow dragging her briefcase. Then like two agile rabbits, they crawled toward an exit at the back of the room.

The spotlight frantically flitted around the room searching for its prey. Waiting until the beam of light crossed over the door where they crouched, Helen pushed the door open. They scuttled through and allowed the door to soundlessly close on its own.

"What do we do?" Martha asked breathlessly. "Where does this lead?"

Helen shook her head, indicating she didn't know where they were, then took out her phone and dialed the police station.

"Helen, I hear someone coming."

Quickly getting up off the floor, they maneuvered the best they could in the dark.

A woman answered Helen's phone call. "Marsden-Lacey Constabulary. Constable Waters speaking. Hold please."

Helen grimaced at the phone and with a flash of brilliance used the phone as a flashlight until they found their way back to the reception area. The huge entry doors had a bulky chain intertwined through the brass handles making the main entrance an impossible escape route.

Unsure what to do or where to go next, they began to panic. Then Helen saw the storage closet for the janitorial staff. Grabbing Martha, she dragged her inside. With cat-like quietness, Martha and Helen concealed themselves in between the mops, brooms and paper towels.

The phone came to life. "Yes? How may we be of help?" the female voice came back on the phone.

Helen said as quietly as possible into the phone, "Get DCI Johns to come over to The Grange."

"I'm sorry Madam but you will need to speak louder," the voice on the other end said loudly.

Helen covered the phone for fear the noise would give them away. Cupping the phone, she persisted, "Listen. I am hiding in a broom closet and being stalked by a homicidal killer. Get DCI Johns over to The Grange right now."

"One moment, please."

Back on hold, Helen heard a Carly Simon song. Appropriately, it was "Anticipation" and it was in its third stanza. Helen held out the phone for Martha to listen. "And these are the good old days" finished up and the chorus began again.

Right then they heard the faint sound of a footstep outside the doorway.

"Madam, are you still there? Madam?" The policewoman's voice sounded like a train horn blaring their location to the crazy person in the corridor.

Martha grabbed the phone and turned the volume all the way to mute. They waited, not daring to move a muscle. Helen's phone flashed a call coming in from the police station.

She hit 'accept' but didn't speak. Muffling her mouth with her hands, she said, being careful to draw out her words. "H—e—l—p. The G—r—a—n—g—e," and then hung up.

Martha reached for Helen's arm and found it. She pulled Helen to her and like a second grade schoolgirl, cupped her hand around her mouth and whispered as softly as possible, "Grab a mop or a broom and something to throw. If it opens the door, throw something and rush it with your mop."

A beam of light flashed through the door crack. Holding whatever cleaning utensils they'd managed to grab, they waited for the inevitable. The delicate sound of a turning latch signaled that someone was twisting the door knob. With every fiber of their bodies tuned and ready to attack, the girls watched as the door inched open.

With a jab to Helen's side, Martha went first, screaming at the top of her lungs, "Ahhh!"

Helen plunged forward into the blinding glare of a flash light yelling, "Ahhh!"

They swung their makeshift weapons wildly in the dark. Finally, they found a sturdy mass to take their blows.

"What the hell is going on? Get them off me!" a man's voice bellowed.

Had the lights come on at that moment, they would have revealed two women, one with a toilet brush and one with an old mop handle, beating a well-built policeman who was trying desperately to fend off their attack.

Helen and Martha had been so keyed up, they didn't slow their attack on the yelling, flailing person in the dark. It was only when strong hands grabbed them and flashlights blinded them, that they finally stood still, holding their cleaning utensils limply by their sides.

"Ladies, calm yourselves. It's the police. We're working to get the lights back on," a male voice said firmly.

Within a few seconds, overhead electric lights flared, bringing the reception area into full illumination. There stood Helen, Martha, and DCI Johns all with disheveled clothes, wild hair and in the case of the two women, slightly crazed looks beginning to melt into simple, "Oh God, what have we done" expressions.

Four uniformed officers were stationed along the wall attempting to maintain their composure at the Chief's ruffled appearance after being attacked by the two terrified, toilet-brush-brandishing women. The officers busied themselves with whatever tasks they could find.

"Take these two and put them in a nice, strong cell at the station," Johns commanded.

"What?" Helen and Martha asked in unison.

He ignored them and pointed to the entrance with a jabbing gesture which indicated to his subordinates to respond to his directions with immediacy.

A woman officer and a middle-aged male officer quickly walked over to Helen and Martha and motioned for them to follow them outside. Johns had already walked away in the direction of the library.

"Wait!" Martha yelled after him. "Don't you want to know what happened to us in there?"

Johns turned around and took a solid stance in the hallway. He compressed his lips tightly in an expression of determination and focused his eyes menacingly on Martha. "Madam, tomorrow I will discuss with you many things, but first you will be treated to a private accommodation, a simple meal and a lumpy cot compliments of the Marsden-Lacey Constabulary."

And with that announcement, DCI Johns turned on his heels and walked like a bull-dog into the library.

Once Martha and Helen were firmly ensconced in the back of a police car and rolling toward the village and their confinement, Helen turned to Martha and said, "Your instincts stink."

"Yeah?" Martha asked truculently.

"Yeah." Helen said firmly.

Chapter 23

Marsden-Lacey's Constabulary was not a typical police station. It was housed in a honey-colored stone building built in the late Georgian period. Due to the efforts of two past inmates who needed to keep busy and recognized the desperate need to improve the aesthetics of the place, the building's facade and surrounding garden was now a picture postcard image of the best architecture and horticulture England had on offer. Flower baskets, climbing roses and tidy garden beds full of flowering plants and shrubs gave the constabulary a decided edge each year when the Marsden-Lacey Garden Club selected a winner for the Best Curb Appeal Award.

It hadn't always been so. Four years ago the station's charm had dwindled to an all-time low and was in serious need of a pick-me-up. Along came the two aforementioned horticultural enthusiasts, Perigrine Clarke and Alistair Turner.

While being held in connection with a counterfeiting crime ring, Perigrine and Alistair quickly became bored sitting in their cells and requested to be allowed to work on the garden beds around the station. Chief Johns, first shackled then allowed them to work wherever they pleased. They were dedicated gardeners.

Their work won them the coveted Lord Litton Village Improvement Award that year and due to their success, they were allowed to attend the ceremony on a day-out pass accompanied by Chief Johns, also a gardening enthusiast.

Only once did Perigrine and Alistair toy with the idea of escape. Their award and their excellent behavior earned them a great deal of freedom about the station. It was this freedom that worked on their minds. They'd conceived the plan for a new pave-stone path wrapping around the constabulary and working its way out to the back parking area. As the developing path reached the outer limits of the garden, it was Alistair who gave voice to the thought in both their minds: "Perry, dear, we've been toiling away on this garden for nearly six months and I'm getting antsy. Lets hop the wall."

"Not this time, Alistair." Perigrine said laying down his spade. "I've been thinking the same thing and I'm pretty sure we've both jumped on this pave-stone idea because we're feeling dull. We can't make a run for it. I want to go straight…at least for the time being."

That's exactly what they did. Once their sentence was up, they bought the garden center next door and continued to maintain the constabulary's plants partly because they were community-service-minded ex-criminals but also because it adjoined their garden center and they didn't want an eyesore to detract from their own exquisitely maintained grounds.

Fortunately for the village, most crime was limited to a few muggings, petty thefts, shoplifting, and vandalism. The current murder at The Grange and the attack on Piers Cousins sent the village into a tizzy of gossiping and speculation. Everyone was enjoying themselves discussing the threats to their lives and recounting the grisly story until no one could have given a fair account of the actual happenings if they'd been asked to. On the plus side, the lurking, homicidal menace was actually bringing people closer together.

Needless to say, DCI Johns couldn't go anywhere without being asked how his investigation was going by the more polite denizens or chided and teased by the scrappier villagers. But because most, including the young toughs, respected their Chief Inspector, they had confidence in his abilities and felt secure in their homes at night for the most part.

It was into this quaint and attractive police station that Helen and Martha were incarcerated following their frightful experience at The Grange. Their stay was uneventful and in fact, the station was quite comfortable and homey.

Constable Waters, an extremely intelligent mother of two young boys, saw to their every need. She made them tea and shared some of the homemade lemon bread she'd brought in to the office that day.

Since there weren't any other boarders for the night besides Sam, Martha's marketplace mugger and Helen and Martha, Constable Waters doubled up the pillows and blankets for the girls' cots and loaned them some of her fashion magazines from her own stash she kept under her desk.

At about eight the next morning there was a knock then a rattle of the bolt on the girls' cell doors.

"Time to wake up, ladies," Constable Waters called out brightly. "DCI Johns wants to see you in about twenty minutes. He's had your breakfasts sent up from his mother, Polly. Looks delicious."

The door opened to Martha's cell and there stood Helen looking tidy as usual.

"I'm starving," Martha said. "I've probably lost ten pounds since this affair began. Hmm, maybe fighting crime works for losing weight."

Helen was quiet so Martha thought she might still be a bit peevish about being locked up all night.

They walked down the hall to a hopefully delicious breakfast. Once they were alone in the interrogation room and Donna (Constable Waters) left to fetch their meals, Helen, facing Martha across a small wooden table, hurriedly said in a low voice, "Don't mention the manuscript yet, okay?"

"Why?" Martha asked looking a bit perplexed by the necessity of withholding such an unconnected piece of information from the Chief.

"I want a chance to look it over. Please wait and pray no one has ransacked your car," Helen pleaded in a whisper.

"What do you think it is?"

"I think it is something fantastically rare and…"

Helen hesitated but Martha pushed her saying, "Yeah, you think it's rare? But what?"

"Well, I wasn't sure if we should relinquish it yet."

"No problem," Martha said. It was the least she could do since she'd thoroughly messed up last night with the instinct thing. "We'll need to explain ourselves about being in The Grange last night. Johns is probably still absolutely furious with us."

They didn't get a chance to finish their conversation because the door swung open and there stood DCI Johns looking at them with a sour expression suggesting he hadn't slept much last night. Over one eye was a small adhesive bandage. Both Helen and Martha cringed outwardly as it triggered memories of attacking the Chief.

"So, let me see," he said as he entered the room and placed a covered plate before each of them, "contaminating a crime scene, assaulting an officer, removing evidence from a crime scene, and these are just a few of the things I'm charging you with as of last night."

DCI Johns smiled and sat down, making himself comfortable on one of the other chairs at the table. He took a bite of his own breakfast, a substantial piece of Constable Waters' lemon bread.

Martha put her head in her hands and moaned while Helen's face was more like a stroke victim's in that she seemed completely unresponsive.

After a few long moments, Martha recovered herself and asked, "Removing evidence? What evidence did we remove?"

"You removed a laptop from Mr. Cousins' house and took it to him at the hospital. You took a piece of cloth from its location on the garden wall. Removing it, handling it and basically contaminating the scene, did you not?"

"Was that wrong?" Helen asked. "We gave the cloth to you."

"Yes, that was wrong!" bellowed Johns. "So wrong that I've given thought to charging you and requesting your bail be set at the highest possible limit. Your actions may have allowed for important evidence to be lost in a homicide case."

Martha and Helen practically swayed in their chairs from Johns' angry blast.

Martha recovered first and came back at him. "We understand but you've got to stop yelling. My head is swirling and I can't think without coffee."

He took a few deep breaths and glared at Martha and Helen. Then, making a noticeable effort, he continued more gently. "So, out of curiosity, why did you take the laptop to Cousins in the hospital and why did you go to The Grange last night?"

Helen and Martha exchanged glances.

Martha jumped in. "We picked up the laptop because Piers requested it when we visited him at the hospital and as for being in The Grange last night, Helen needed her briefcase with her laptop and her phone charger. Surely, that isn't a crime to retrieve things that are rightly yours in the first place."

"It is, Mrs. Littleword, in this instance, it most definitely is," Johns said with a touch of sarcasm in his voice. "You see, the entire area is off-limits to anyone until we open it back up again to the public. If you'd wanted something, you should have called the station and an officer would have been dispatched to accompany you into The Grange and help you locate your necessary items. As for the laptop, if I remember right, there was a piece of yellow tape across Piers Cousins' study door. Hmm, that means 'No Admittance' to even the simplest of minds."

The little nerve above Martha's eyebrow twitched. Something deep inside her told her to not look up from her tea mug. Instead she took a deep breath and fought to maintain her composure. At that moment all she wanted to do was hit him right in the stomach but instead she lifted her chin and gave him a square look and a thin smile.

"Well," she said quietly, "the yellow tape wasn't there when we simple folk returned to Healy."

"Yes, that's right." Helen joined in. "There wasn't yellow tape anywhere. Martha is right. It didn't occur to us we were doing anything wrong."

Johns stared at them for a few moments. "You must have considered that the laptop was an important piece of evidence."

"Then why didn't you remove it the night Piers was shot?" Helen asked.

"We didn't need to. Cousins said during our interview at Healy the videos could be accessed from any computer as long as you had the web address and the password. He was supposed to come by the station the following day but of course he was shot. Couldn't get the password until he was able to give it to us. So, the laptop was left in situ."

"Then what difference does it make if we took the laptop to Piers?" they both asked in unison.

He stirred his tea. "Because, not everyone would have known that last bit and might have wanted to get hold of the laptop to see if they might manipulate the videos including Cousins." He stared into his mug then raised his gaze to look at the girls.

"It wasn't us," Helen firmly stated. "And I don't think it was Piers either."

"The point is, ladies, someone did. Your messing around in this case is about to get you in legal trouble and more importantly, if you don't stop, possibly dead."

The room became quiet as all three people considered this last remark.

"We needed to see from those videos, if they were manipulated and when. Cousins is still on our list of suspects. As for the piece of cloth you found, it's special. It can limit the amount of residue that remains on someone's hands when they fire a gun. Someone thought this attempted murder out. They also knew you were going to The Grange. Who knew you were going to be there last night?"

The only two people they had told were Piers and Louis Devry.

"You want to tell me about what happened last night?" he asked gently.

Helen lifted the silver lid from her breakfast plate. The steam wafted up and she took in the lovely smell of sausages, a slice of quiche and a small bowl of melon. Martha followed suit. Johns watched both women delicately begin to eat.

Helen put her fork down after two bites. "We wanted to get my things from the library and…"

She stopped. Martha could tell Helen was struggling with something. Johns was waiting. Helen took a deep breath and a quick look at Martha. She seemed to make up her mind and began again. "Mrs. Thyme wanted us to deliver a package to Piers but it somehow got lodged under the car seat. We didn't find it again until we got back to The Grange. Martha recognized that it might be the envelope Devry took out of Carstons' hand in the video."

"So, you've also seen the videos," Johns stated.

They both nodded without words.

"Then what happened?"

"Well, I realized the manuscript inside must be something unusual from looking at it briefly in the car, but I needed my gloves, glasses, and laptop to better study it. We put it back under the seat and found our way around the building. Everything was fine until we got into the library and the lights went out. This horrible voice came from nowhere and we panicked."

"Horrible voice? What did it sound like?"

Martha came alive. "It sounded like someone talking into a voice modulator. Something kids play with to make their voices sound silly or creepy."

"We crawled under the library table. Whoever it was had a flashlight that kept scanning the room. Martha pushed the bookshelves over which gave us a distraction to escape. We made our way out the side door on our knees and in the dark. Our cell phone gave us some light and we got into the janitorial closet where we called the station for help," Helen finished.

Martha looked at Johns. "How did you get there so fast?"

"We were already on our way. We have The Grange electronically monitored now. The constable taking your call was asked to keep you as long as possible on the phone." Johns was quiet for a moment. "You two must have been followed because it was the side door that signaled to us first. That was the one you entered through. It was the service entrance that signaled second which was about five minutes after the side door signaled."

The Chief screwed up his forehead, pursed his lips, then gave his verdict. "Someone is following you, girls. Someone either knows you have something they want or thinks you know something they wish you didn't. Either way, you're in it deep and it's deadly."

Chapter 24

To send his point home, Chief Johns returned Martha and Helen to their cells for what he called safe keeping. He told Constable Waters they'd be spending another night and not to allow them visitors. Besides, he needed the bookish one to give him a briefing on the contents of the envelope which was supposedly stuffed under a car seat in Martha's Mini Cooper.

He marched out to the back lot where they kept impounded vehicles. There was Martha's green car. Foresight along with years of experience told him not to leave anything behind last night. He'd not only collected the Mini Cooper but also picked up Helen's briefcase.

The car door was locked but not a problem for the person with the keys. He'd finally obtained them by threatening Martha with a strip search if she didn't hand them over. That had been fun, he thought to himself with a smile.

Digging under the driver's seat, he found nothing. Next, he felt under the passenger's seat and touched something made out of material. He pulled it out and to his surprise found himself holding a red, lacy bra. Johns' eyebrows arched quizzically as he held the item out for inspection.

"What on earth does that woman do when she drives around in her car?" he mumbled out loud.

Thinking to himself he should probably have her monitored, he shoved the bra back under the seat and stuck his head down close to the floor board to get a better look. Nothing. Wait, there back behind what appeared to be a box of feminine hygiene products, he saw a manila envelope. He shook his head. She'd definitely tried to booby-trap the hiding place.

Straightening up to his full height, he worked to open the envelope. Inside, he saw a thick bundle of bound papers enclosed in a heavy plastic bag.

"Better get back to the nice-tempered one and see what she can make of this," he thought to himself. With the envelope in hand, he walked back to the station musing on the red lacy number he'd found under Martha's seat. Two sets of curious eyes watch his departure while paying particular attention to the package gripped firmly in Johns' right hand.

Scene break

"Alistair," Perigrine said, "you know how I get that itchy feeling in my palms when we're close to something deliciously valuable?"

"Yes, P. I do." Alistair was lounging comfortably, legs crossed at the knees in his Bergere chair and reading an E.F. Benson anthology of ghost stories.

"Our Chief Inspector has something…" Perigrine studied the envelope dangling from Johns' hand as he walked across the parking lot.

Alistair never interrupted Perigrine while he was tuning into the universal money mind. Given enough time, P. would sift through the incoming impulses which would guide him to an understanding of what was causing his palms to itch. His intuition never missed the mark. Everyone had a talent and Perigrine's was knowing when he was close to something extremely valuable.

"I think it should be sussed out, Ally. I'm on my way to Harriet's to get a cake. I think you might need to prune the roses near the Chief's window. They need to be taken into hand. See you in a bit." Perigrine removed his work apron, flung it on an untidy desk and made some quick adjustments to his bow tie in a mirror hung below a picture of The Queen.

Confident his appearance was in order, he strode out of the office toward the High Street and the best tea cakes one could buy in Marsden-Lacey.

129

Chapter 25

"I can't be sure of course. We need to have it looked at by an expert. Someone like Louis Devry obviously would know," Helen said. She'd been delicately studying the manuscript Johns retrieved from Martha's car.

"What does it look like in your less-expert opinion?" Johns asked.

Martha rolled her eyes. "Nice."

Johns winked at her like he knew something incriminating about her.

Taken aback and a bit perplexed by his new tone, Martha scowled.

Helen didn't seem to take it as an insult and replied, "It's nineteenth century and in a woman's hand. There's negligible deterioration which means its been well cared for in a collection where there were proper environmental conditions maintained. It's a novel. Beautifully written. Almost poetic in its style. What I find curious is the envelope containing the manuscript is American made and the mylar casing is museum grade but the style of writing is English. I've not seen the entire list of The Grange's holdings so I'm not sure whether this may be in their collection or not. We need to show it to Mr. Devry."

"That can be arranged," Johns said.

"Chief Inspector Johns," Martha began in an upbeat, professional tone, "Helen and I need to negotiate our situation."

Johns asked with an unenthusiastic smile, "Oh?"

"Yes, you see, we'll stay out of your investigation if you would please let us return to work. As you can well imagine, being held by the police doesn't do well with my employer or Helen's clients."

"Mrs. Littleword, you may not realize the danger you're in at this moment. Someone has a bone to pick with both of you."

"We realize the danger but we plan to stay at my house and if you might consider our arrest to be more of the house variety, then I might get to keep my job and Helen can arrange to do her work from there."

"Are you suggesting I should find it in to my operating budget to pay for personal police protection for two American ladies who don't know how to keep their noses out of trouble?"

Helen spoke up. "Chief Inspector, we would like to see all the paper work you've done so far regarding our offenses and our incarceration."

Johns frowned. If they were going to play that card, he'd have to let them go. He hadn't created any documentation regarding their supposed offenses because he knew they were harmless. But being too nosey was turning out to be dangerous and he wanted to put some fear into them.

He put on a grave face. "Ladies, I haven't documented anything because I think you're harmless nit-whits who are likely to get themselves in trouble if they don't leave the investigating to the professionals."

Both women stiffened at the insult. Johns continued.

"You can go. But if you poke even one tiny toe into my investigation again, you'll be serving your time at Broadmore in North Yorkshire. Not a fun vacation destination for nice ladies like yourselves." He smiled wickedly and blinked a number of times staring directly at them.

Helen lifted herself regally and smiled coldly. Her rigid shoulders and composed pleasantness made her look like an ice princess who was ready to dismiss the commoners from her presence. "Thank you, Chief Inspector. We'll be respectful of your case and if anything should come our way, we promise to come to you directly."

Martha was busy spraying perfume on her neck she'd found in her jacket pocket. Johns smelled the wafting rose scent and turned to see her squirt a low shot down her shirt and into her bosom.

He felt his mind soar aloft like a balloon released by a child at the park. Martha looked up and saw instantly his eyes slightly glazed over. With typical Martha flair, she tossed him the same impish smile she'd given him earlier except she added a knowing wink.

An electric shock hit Johns in the chest and sizzled around his whole being until it discharged through each individual rigid hair on his buzzed head.

Martha, waiting for the most opportune moment, coyly tucked the perfume back into her favorite place, her cleavage, and watched with obvious glee as Johns shuffled papers hurriedly.

"Okay then," he said hoarsely, "I'll have Constable Waters assist you with gathering your things and getting your car out of the impound lot."

The Chief pushed the thought of the red, lacy item under the car seat out of his mind. He knew without any hesitation this Southern redhead was getting under his skin and, for comfort's sake, he couldn't be in the room with her one more second.

Chapter 26

Alistair, hidden as he was behind the magnificent English rose bushes flanking the west side of the Constabulary, heard their entire conversation. He also saw the manuscript laying on the table, left tantalizingly unprotected by the departing Chief and the two women.

While Alistair and Perigrine were working all those months on the Constabulary, they'd learned many valuable things about the place, things like how Chief Johns' office was a treasure trove of fine whiskeys secreted in ladies handbags, and how staff office windows weren't regularly locked.

The room Helen, Martha and Johns had met was called the interrogation/lunch room, better known to the constables as the break room. It was housed on the first floor with easy access through its window. Alistair managed to pop the latch of the window and slip inside in less time most people take opening their refrigerator door. Being an affectionate soul, he thought it would be nice if Perigrine could peruse the manuscript for a little while, then they would return it. No harm done. He lifted the mylar bag with the manuscript still enclosed, and left the same way he'd entered.

With a jaunty high step, Alistair crossed the back lot of the Constabulary and made his way to the Garden Centre and the attached home he shared with his best friend, Perigrine.

Scene break

"Yes, Chief, I'll see the manuscript and give you my opinion," Louis Devry said softly into the phone.

"Helen Ryes believes you would be the perfect person to tell us what we have or if it's already a piece of The Grange's collection. I feel certain it may be an important part of our story regarding Sir Carstons," Johns said.

Devry assured Johns he would be at the station by midday and put the phone down on the side table beside his bed. A crippling pressure crept up his legs and arms. Squeezing each joint vengefully and knowingly like a cruel devil bent on torturing him incrementally, it finally reached the center of his body plunging him into a complete and petrifying anxiety attack.

They'd found the manuscript. How in the world had they found it? He'd gone crazy looking for it the night of the garden party. Someone removed it from under his mattress. How would he answer for it?

Breathing rapidly with his heart pounding and the muscles of his chest tightening, he forced himself to think about her: Emilia. The anxiety attacks always made him feel like he was dying. Slipping away into a cruel madness.

He brought his mind slowly around again to focus on the manuscript. Who took it from his room? If only Carstons hadn't shown up Friday then he would have had more time to situate it into The Grange's collection. Last week had been a walk in Hell. The trip to the States, terrified he would be caught removing the manuscript from the Harvard archives and then there was Carissa's health. Carstons' threat to expose him almost put an end to his plan, but someone fortunately killed him instead.

Announcing his find of the manuscript to the world would have made him a celebrity. He would have been an overnight academic success story. The world had no idea the manuscript even existed. It hadn't been catalogued correctly all those years ago and when he had found it while working in the archives of The Treasure Room, he knew it was his ticket to a name for himself.

His chest constricted again. Everything was going wrong. Louis made himself think of Emilia. Like a tranquilizer, her memory turned the tide on the thunderous fear eating at his mind and crippling his body.

The dream of making a name for himself was over. Someone took the book from the hiding place and they would know he was a fraud. He looked at the ceiling and wished for death. Loneliness and a quiet room were the only echoes to his wish.

Reaching for the Klonopin on his side table, he hoped it would help to calm him down. The pill would bring the anxiety attack under control and allow him to act normally with the Chief later when they met. On the bedside table, he set the alarm on his phone to wake him in case he fell asleep. Then taking two pills, even though he was only supposed to take one each day, he lay back on his pillows and let his thoughts return to Emilia.

One last thing passed through his mind before the drug took affect: it was odd how the bedroom door sucked shut suddenly. It only did that when another door opened somewhere else in the house, but he didn't have time to consider it any further because the medicine sent him deep into a sleep.

He was completely unaware when someone entered the room, saw him sleeping, then read the label on his medicine bottle. The visitor helped him take the rest of the pills and for good measure, washed them down with Scotch.

A quick note saying, "I can't go on. I killed Carstons," was scratched out in a rough hand to disguise its provenance.

With the gentleness of a kiss blown by a wicked fairy, Devry got what he wished for and someone else got a scapegoat.

Scene Break

After a delicious lunch at Harriet's, Perigrine returned home with a poppyseed cake to hand deliver later to the constabulary. He picked up his "English Home" magazine and adjusted his bow tie. It was time for a short rest then off to talk with Donna.

Alistair watched how Perigrine was really enjoying himself for the first time in two years. He knew P. was feeling his creative and analytical mind working on something tinged with adventure, or larceny, depending on your perspective.

Once done mentally critiquing the houses in the magazine, he turned to Alistair and said briskly, "Well, dear Ally, did you hear anything of interest today?"

"No," was Alistair's simple, flat answer. He'd decided to keep his earlier acquisition a secret until this coming Friday.

Friday was the day Perigrine did the financials and he was always fussing about Ally's "spending issues," as he liked to call them. Alistair had been very bad this week. He'd bought a gorgeous moonlit landscape done in oil at an estate sale handled by Selkirks. It was an exquisite thing. He truly believed he was saving the beautiful piece from the clutches of riffraff who wouldn't appreciate it properly. It was completely out of Alistair's budget and would, if P. found out about it, send Perigrine on a tiresome rampage about money and self control.

So, Alistair decided to be coy about hearing anything during his pruning time at the constabulary. He'd managed to get hold of something that would balance the budget completely with Perigrine and send him into a whirlwind of delight, therefore forgiving the purchase of the costly landscape. Alistair would wait for the right moment to spring it.

"I'm going to drop off the cake I purchased from Harriet's and talk to Donna about the item I saw Johns carrying earlier," Perigrine said putting the magazine down on a side table.

"Good. You know, the Chief was talking with two women while I was pruning." He added the two-handed gesture for quotation marks for effect. "They were in a meeting of sorts studying a book. Didn't look like anything important though. Nothing you would be interested in." He trailed off while feigning to work on a sudoku puzzle.

"Alistair. What did you see exactly?" Perigrine said jumping forward to sit on the edge of the chair.

Alistair assumed the character of the oblivious cohort. "Johns with two women talking about a book. One said it was 19th century, handwritten and a novel. They thought the new curator at the museum, Devry somebody, should look at it."

136

Perigrine relaxed back in his chair thoughtfully gazing at the perfectly manicured back garden of their house and the delicate stone sculpture of the Grecian goddess, Melpomene. She held a mask and gazed down into a quiet koi pond the boys had constructed as a serenity feature for their garden. He and Ally had plumbed the mask so that water poured out of its mouth and into the water pool below. Melpomene ruled her small kingdom with grace.

The manuscript must have been in the envelope he saw Johns carrying across the parking lot and it must have been the same book Alistair heard the women and Johns discussing. A certain anxiousness took over Perigrine. The Muse, Melpomene, in the garden didn't take her eyes off the ceaselessly swimming koi. A fantastic thought creeped in upon his musings.

Getting up from his chair, Perigrine walked out the back door like one who is hypnotized. He left a bewildered Alistair reclining on a sofa and watching as he made his way through the garden gate carrying a small teacake in the direction of the Marsden-Lacey Constabulary.

Chapter 27

"What happened to the book?" Johns asked at the top of his lungs.

Constable Waters and Constable Cross came running from opposite corners of the station.

There on the table lay the empty manila envelope, no manuscript anywhere.

"We only left the room five minutes ago," he continued to bellow with an increasingly crimson face.

"Sir, no one else has been in the building," Constable Waters offered.

"That's right, Sir. I've been up at the front desk and it's been so quiet today. Only staff has been here unless you consider the two women you showed out," Cross added.

"Go bring them back here. Now!" Johns demanded so loudly that both Cross and Waters jumped. "Go!"

Both constables hurried from the room and out to the parking lot where they found Helen and Martha trying to bring the Mini Cooper through the impound lot. They waved the ladies over and asked with remarkable composure if they would please return to the station.

The girls shrugged, got out of the car and followed Constable Waters back into the building while Constable Cross searched the car.

Chief Johns waited for them in the lobby. His face was red with an irascible, angry bulldog look about it.

"What's the problem now?" Martha asked followed by a sigh as she put her purse down on one of the waiting room chairs.

"Mrs. Littleword and Mrs. Ryes, Constable Waters would like to see you ladies individually in a dressing room," Johns said.

"What's this all about?" Helen demanded.

"The book is gone," he replied. "Disappeared right after you two left the room."

In perfect unison they both hotly denied, "It wasn't us. We didn't take it."

"That is yet to be seen." He jabbed in the direction of the dressing rooms with a pointed finger.

"I cannot believe this. You actually believe we would steal that book? Where in the world do you think we have it hidden on our bodies?" Helen asked with both hands on her hips.

Martha stood there glowering at Johns with her arms crossed. "Helen, he thinks we've stuffed it in our undergarments."

Johns gave Martha a sour, tight-lipped look then jerked his head in the direction of the dressing rooms, indicating Waters should get on with the job.

"Fine. You may strip us bare, if that's what it takes to be freed from this place, Helen declared like a spirited suffragette who was about to be mishandled by the cretinous police.

Constable Waters showed them each to a dressing room and, with an apologetic tone, said, "I'm sorry, but you will have to disrobe and put on the gowns. Please leave your things on the table and then take a chair. I'll be right back."

They continued to complain and plot revenge the entire time they were in the rooms but in the end, they complied. Constable Waters returned and smiled kindly at them. She looked through their things with a gentle hand.

Turning to them she said compassionately, "You may put your things on and come out to the waiting area when you're ready."

The entire process took half an hour for both of them to disrobe, be inspected and redress themselves. Once out in the lobby, they waited impatiently to hear if they could leave.

"Mrs. Littleword and Mrs. Reyes, please follow me," Constable Waters asked.

Back down the hall again they went. Donna showed them into the Chief's office where he was sitting behind his desk drinking a cup of coffee and glaring at a computer screen.

"Ladies," he started in a more hospitable tone once he saw they were standing at his door, "please come in. You understand we have to be certain you didn't have the manuscript."

Originally, they'd decided to give the Chief a piece of their mind, but with his unexpected reversal in approach, they found themselves without recourse but to be understanding. Still wanting to go home, they knew antagonizing him wouldn't serve their cause.

He continued. "We're studying our security cameras positioned around the station and they show a man crawling out of the interview room window. We'll find him, but again, please accept my apology for having a brusque manner earlier."

"It might have been nice to check the surveillance videos first," Martha said, still miffed by the search.

Helen held up her hand to quiet Martha who sighed dramatically.

"Will you please let me know if you find the manuscript? I have a strong feeling it's something special," Helen said.

"Of course, Mrs. Reyes. I've set an appointment to meet with Louis Devry today. Unfortunately, I'll need to cancel it, but as soon as we know something, I'll get a message to you." He dug in his desk. Finding a toffee, he popped it into his mouth.

Martha turned to go. "If that's all then, we'll be on our way." She was in a hurry to check on her pets.

The girls left the Chief giving orders about getting someone to go over to Louis Devry's house since he wasn't answering his phone.

Helen and Martha found the Mini Cooper parked in front of the station and without looking back, drove directly to Flower Pot Cottage and its two hungry, crabby pets.

Scene Break

Piers Cousins was terribly relieved to be out from under the watchful and matronly care of Nurse Davis. He cringed slightly while remembering the last couple of days. Davis' daily sponge baths were a difficult memory to free himself of. She must have confused him with a rabbit she wanted to skin. There were moments when he thought he saw a gleam in her eye while she scrubbed his legs to a ruby redness.

To be fair though, she checked on him often, fussed over his pillows and monitored his diet and bowel movements with zeal. It was this ever-present care that lead to his urgent desire to get out of the place at any cost.

When he finally saw his doctor, a woman in her early thirties, she reluctantly agreed to let him leave the hospital as long as he checked in with his general practitioner in a few days to make sure all was healing correctly. Within minutes of the papers being signed, he made his way outside and found a taxi.

As the vehicle weaved its way through the traffic, Piers thought about the surveillance video and wondered if his long-time friend, Louis, was Sir Carstons' killer.

Louis had denied killing Carstons but who else had such excellent motives? There was his love for Emilia and the terrible way Carstons, her husband, treated her. To be fair, Piers thought, that could be one of his own motives for wanting Carstons dead.

Louis also admitted to him that Carstons was trying to bully him into turning a blind eye while Carstons stole items from the collection. In return for Louis' silence, Carstons would stay quiet about the details of Louis losing his job at Harvard, a typical Carstons' low-life maneuver.

The view out Piers' backseat window showed they were reaching the outer fringes of Marsden-Lacey. He considered the story Louis told him at the hospital yesterday as he watched the countryside roll before him in all its summer glory. Remembering Emilia's effect on almost any man who came in contact with her, Piers thought of Louis' love for her. He thought of his own love for her.

It was only after she married Carstons that Louis finally accepted the role of friend to Emilia. No one could understand what Emilia saw in Alan Carstons. Before he married her, Carstons must have spread the charm on thick. He was capable of being whatever he needed to be to achieve his own ends.

Only Emilia's pregnancy ended Louis' desire to stay close. Louis never knew about Piers' affair with Emilia or that the child she bore was Piers'.

Louis' visit to the hospital and his confession about Carstons blackmailing him hadn't shocked Piers. Anything that Carstons did quit shocking Piers years ago. Carstons was forever manipulating people to get what he wanted and if that meant blackmail or cruelty, then so be it.

If there was more to Louis' story, Piers would have to find out. One thing was for sure, Louis was ferocious in the video when he snatched the satchel from Carstons' grasp and pointed for him to get out. If he decided later to kill him, what was the final motivating factor?

Feeling tired, Piers shut his eyes and lay back against the taxi's seat. After a few minutes, he opened them to see they'd taken the road leading to the High Street of Marsden-Lacey. Impulsively, he called out to the driver to take him to an alternative address instead. Potter Cottage on Pike Lane was Louis' cottage. Maybe it was time to see if his old friend needed a lawyer. He would gladly help Louis Devry, even if he was Carstons' killer. In fact, he thought to himself, he actually owed him a debt of gratitude.

The taxi stopped and Piers jumped out. He paid the driver and told him to wait. Finding the doorbell, he pushed the button hearing the chimes ring through the house within. No one came. He could see Louis' Volvo parked in the adjoining shed so he knew Louis must be home.

Piers walked around the house, peering in the windows one after another. The house was eerily quiet not even a bird or bee disturbed its slumber. A final room near the back of the house with a window close to the ground allowed Piers to see into the space inside. He pressed his face against the pane of glass, shielding his eyes from the glare of the reflection. There, lying on the bed, was Louis perfectly asleep.

Piers rapped at the window and yelled, "Louis! Wake up. We need to talk."

Not a twinge of movement came from the man. Piers banged and called again but nothing, no response. A dark idea began to take form in his mind. The picture through the bedroom window was wrong. With a sudden knowledge that he was seeing a dead man, his friend, Piers bolted back around the cottage to the front door. He signaled to the taxi driver who rolled down his window.

"Call an ambulance! I think the man inside is sick. Hurry!"

With a great run at the door, he rammed through it easily and made his way to where Louis was lying in the room at the end of the hall. Once there, Piers stood above the quiet, fully-dressed figure of his friend lying on the bed. He tried to fight his own fear and calm himself enough to study the scene.

With his heart beating rapidly, he reached out to touch Louis but froze instead. Louis' chest wasn't expanding and contracting like someone breathing normally. No respiration was taking place. This combined with a medicine bottle laying in Louis' limp hand, made Piers suddenly desperate to do something. He laid his head on Louis' chest trying to hear something, anything. Not a sound came from his old friend's heart. It was still as death.

A chill crept up Piers' skin. He backed away from the bed and the peaceful corpse then slumped into a nearby chair. The first thought that eked into his mind was how Louis was with Emilia now. It was what Louis had always wanted.

The sound of sirens moving toward the cottage and then footsteps coming down the hallway stirred him to action. He stood up as two paramedics pushed into the room. Piers pointed to the bed. They quickly focused their attention on the body. Gloves on, they conversed with each other only, while working on the lifeless body. Piers heard another set of sirens coming up the road to the cottage.

Soon a constable was in the room asking questions of the two paramedics. Feeling detached as if he was watching the scene from a remote place, Piers' emotions were dammed by the shock.

From the back of the house he heard a gruff and familiar voice. Chief Johns' presence preceded him and then, in his take-charge manner, he stalked into the room. He looked tired but determined, and his gaze bore down on Piers.

"You find him?" he asked.

Piers' brain snapped-to. "Yes," was all he could get out before Johns stopped him with another question.

"Why are you here?"

"I wanted to talk with him about something."

"What?"

Piers' rattled brain wouldn't process. He forced it to focus. Johns was staring at him, waiting. Finally, he found himself wondering if it was the right moment to say he suspected Louis of killing Carstons. "I...I...Well, you see, I wanted to ask Louis if he killed Carstons."

There it was. The truth he'd kept in his mind but had't wanted to say out loud. It was said in the same manner as a child, blurting out his thoughts and then wondering at the audibility of his statement.

"Oh?" was all Johns said in return. He scrutinized Piers' face and waited for more.

"I mean that I came by out of concern. I needed to know what Carstons had on him."

Johns cocked his head and regarded the affluent, well-dressed man. Then as abruptly as he entered, he walked back out leaving Piers to stare after him.

Scene Break

Piers stood quietly waiting to be told what to do. He heard people coming and going in the house, and other vehicles' tires crunching to a stop outside the cottage. He wondered if he should leave the room. It was beginning to make him feel claustrophobic and nauseous.

Johns bustled back into the room and addressed Piers. "Need you to come outside Mr. Cousins, if you would. We need to get our forensic team in here and I need to find a place for us to talk. I'm sure you have some things you would like to get off your chest."

"Yes. Thank you," Piers said like a man waking from a dream. But then he asked with force, "May I make a phone call?"

"Sure. Come find me in the front hall when you're finished and we can start."

Johns turned and began talking with the forensic team's leader.

Piers walked free of the tight bedroom. He could actually feel something tugging, clinging and pulling on his spirit as if it wasn't ready for him to leave yet. As he walked toward the open door leading to the outside world humming with life, he could feel the band stretching to its breaking point. It snapped, releasing him as he stepped out through the front door of the cottage and into the summer sunlight.

Taking a deep breath with his eyes shut, he let it out slowly. Birds were singing and bees were humming in the flowering shrubs surrounding the cottage. The air smelled of rain and, needing to talk to someone kind, he dialed Helen's number.

Chapter 28

Constable Waters had been left in charge of the constabulary while the rest of the team was either on lunch or working the situation at Potter Cottage. Her morning had been spent dealing with the young man, Sam Berry, who'd mugged Martha Littleword in the market place.

He'd been complaining non-stop to use his mobile phone. His aunt and guardian, Harriet Berry, the owner of the best tea shop in Marsden-Lacey, received his only allowed call from the police station and promptly hung up on him. Sam, for the time being, had run out of sympathetic women to turn to.

In the reception area, Donna was preparing the duty roster while at the same time updating her Facebook page. An "arumph" sound and a shadow on her left hand side startled her. Looking up, she saw Perigrine Clarke smiling like a Cheshire cat while humbly proffering a delicious-looking tea cake across the reception desk.

"Hi, Perigrine," she said warmly with a big smile. "What's this lovely piece of confection you've brought me?"

Perigrine leaned in over the reception desk with the familiar air of a conspiratorial suburban housewife trading savory secrets with the next-door neighbor and said, "Donna, I've had one of my feelings today. It's driving me crazy. Do you have time for tea? It's one of Harriet's cakes."

While Perigrine and Alistair were "guests" at the constabulary, Donna had spent a great deal of time discussing with P. his special ability to sense things or guess the future. They'd built a nice friendship. On P.'s part he could warn Donna when one of the boys might be doing something they shouldn't or if her mother-in-law was about to call to announce a visit. Donna reciprocated by convincing Johns that P. and Alistair should have more freedom about the constabulary or maybe a day-out pass to visit their favorite haunts.

"Well, you'd better tell me all about it, Perigrine. Best to get it off your chest. Please say it isn't about one of the children."

"Oh no. Not the boys, dear." He made a waving motion of his hand like he was shooing away a nasty thought.

Then in a theatrical manner meant to elicit a modicum amount of sympathy, he put his right hand up and drummed his fingers above his ear while shaking his hand lightly enough to convince anyone watching that he was a tiny bit distraught.

Donna wasn't taken in by the performance, but she did love P. for making the effort to give her a taste of his dramatic abilities, so she applied a mask of deep concern and asked what he thought the feeling meant.

"I know something extremely valuable is here. I sensed it yesterday and it's in danger. It traveled a long way and it's been lost for a long time. I can feel it in my bones, Donna. It's almost like it's talking to me. Is there any way I can see it?" Perigrine begged.

The look on Donna's face would have been "Liked" by at least ten of her closest friends because rarely did she look so completely shocked. Her mouth slack-jawed and her eyes wide with disbelief, she mentally processed whether Perigrine was trying to get information or if he was actually on the up and up. Donna wasn't the type to be at a loss for words, but Perigrine's timing was unbelievable. Was it possible he actually knew something?

"Perigrine," she began in the pedantic, firm tone of an exasperated schoolmarm, "you better tell me what you know because you might be in a terrible amount of trouble walking in here and making a statement like that right now."

With an honest look of confusion, Perigrine stopped the theatrics and straightened his tie. Her reaction was completely the opposite of what he'd hoped for so. "What do you mean? Is something amiss?"

147

Poorer choice of words had rarely been used than the last three of P.'s choosing. Donna got up and came around the reception desk and grabbed the astonished six foot, tweed-wearing dandy and dragged him back to the interview room.

Initially, Perigrine put up no resistance and only when he found himself sitting in a metal chair across the desk from Donna did he raise his eyebrows in an effort to regain his composure. He smiled weakly. "Donna? Did I say something wrong?"

"You better come clean, Perigrine. What do you think this something is that is lost? And don't play games with me. This is serious," she said.

P. looked down at the tea cake he'd managed to hang on to while he was being dragged back for questioning to the break room. His mind went back to the scene of Johns walking across the car park with the envelope. With his eyes shut, he searched the impression for what secrets it held. That envelope radiated such a powerful energy to Perigrine that he simply tingled all over. His eyes snapped open and he locked on to Donna's searching gaze.

"Donna," he said with an honest simplicity, "I saw an envelope in Chief Johns' hands while he walked across the car park. Something in it is terribly priceless. I wanted to get my hands on it and probably for all the wrong reasons which is always a sign it must be fabulously valuable. Has something happened surrounding it?"

Donna knew when he was sincere. "Perigrine, I can't discuss anything with you but if you have a connection with this item, will you please be forthcoming and give us any information you might have?" She leaned into the table they shared.

"Donna, what happened? Is it not here anymore?" he asked, horrified, mimicking her movement toward the center of the table.

"P., it went missing this morning about eleven. Don't breathe a word of this to anyone. We've someone on video climbing out of one of the windows. He'll be caught but it might take some time."

On hearing the word "he," to Perigrine's credit, he managed not to express on his face what his mind was flashing in large

148

neon letters. Instead he looked down into his upturned palms and then back into Donna's face. As if she were his confessor, he took a deep sigh and made a clean breast of it.

"Donna, as God is my witness, I did lust after whatever it was in that envelope. But I didn't take it. I didn't. Let me try and help find it. Okay? If I had taken it, you can bet I wouldn't be here. I'd be half way to a shady London dealer."

Donna considered his face. What he said was true about the dealer. If he had it, he wouldn't be showing up with a cake and a tale about his feelings. She gave him the benefit of the doubt.

"Okay, that's true enough, Perigrine. Keep quiet about what I told you and let me know if you find anything out."

Scene Break

Perigrine left the tea cake behind to bring succor to the over-worked constables and to make a small atonement for almost being enticed again down the path of perdition. He left through the front entrance and made a good show of walking toward the High Street but once out of sight of the station, he made a quick detour down Peddlers Alley and back to the Garden Centre and home.

Grateful no one was in the shop, he made a beeline to the back. There in the corner of the office sat Alistair, calmly brushing their contented schnauzer, Comstock, whose tail wagged a friendly hello at Perigrine's arrival.

Giving Alistair enough time to realize his entrance, Perigrine leaned up against the bookshelves and watched as a finished and fluffed Comstock shook himself all over and trotted off to the garden and a likely dirt bath.

Only then did he ask softly, "Ally, my dear, where the Hell is it?"

"Why under the dog's bed of course, Perry. Where else would it be?" Alistair smiled while pouring himself and Perigrine a brandy. "Thought it would make you a nice present. You do work so hard."

Accepting the brandy, Perigrine swirled it around in the tumbler. "Thank you for the thought, but unless you want to rekindle your relationship with the prison board, we'd better get it back somehow. They've got someone on video. Won't take long to put their noses to the ground and find you."

"Oh. What a shame. I had such high hopes for it. How about we drop it into the mail slot and call it a day?" Alistair grinned like an imp then sipped his brandy.

Shaking his head with an affectionate smile, Perigrine Clarke considered his options. The desire for the book was gone but he was still curious to see it. Lifting the dog's bed, he saw an unexciting plastic bag with what appeared to be a bunch of papers inside. Knowing a bit about how to handle delicate works on paper, he gingerly opened the sleeve and peeked inside. The hairs on the back of his neck stood up as the smell of "old" wafted up to his nostrils.

With great reverence he read the first few lines. There was no doubt in Perigrine's mind who'd written those words. It now became a question of national identity and if P. was anything, he was a proud defender of all things British.

Like most good ideas that come from somewhere out of the blue or maybe in this case from providence, P. then had an epiphany and probably saved Alistair from another incarceration and the book from another century of obscurity.

Chapter 29

Helen and Martha found Flower Pot Cottage a welcoming sanctuary. Sitting snugly along the canal with its ivy-covered stone walls and wild, unkempt garden, it seemed to smile and beckon them to retreat within its cozy, safe walls. They immediately took steaming hot showers, put on clean flannel pajamas and dove into the creamy clam chowder and crusty french bread they bought at Harriet's Shop after leaving the station.

Making themselves separate nests of blankets and bed pillows, one on the sofa for Helen and another for Martha in her favorite big chair and ottoman, they surrendered to the drowsy warmth of the pleasant room. With an old Peter Sellers "Pink Panther" movie playing on the television, they were enjoying a few laughs when the phone rang.

"Don't answer it," Martha said as she scratched Gus' ears.

"What if it's important? Could be your daughter."

"She would call my mobile. It's not work either. I called in to take the day off. Might be Johns though." Martha winked.

"Then answer it," Helen said with a twinkle in her eye.

"No. You get it. Don't want to make it easy for him."

"Oh, good Lord. Fine."

Helen threw off her blanket and picked her way past the pillows, tea mugs and soup bowls to find the phone still ringing but hidden under a karate magazine.

"Do you read this stuff?"

Martha shrugged. "I'm learning to kill with my bare hands. Remember? You might be surprised to know that I'm on my orange belt."

Helen rolled her eyes and tapped the phone's 'On' button.

"Hello?"

Martha watched and listened to Helen make soothing comments into the phone like "Oh my" and "Oh how terrible."

Finally, she said, "Piers, come straight over to Martha's cottage. We'll put on the tea. I think you could use a cup. Yes, Flower Pot Cottage. It's near the canal not far from the first lock. We'll be here."

Putting the phone down, she turned to Martha who sat in her comfy chair with a sour look on her face petting both the dog and cat.

"There's been a death, Martha. Louis Devry is dead."

Gus and Martha stared blankly back at Helen.

"Did you hear what I said? Louis Devry is dead. Piers is terribly shaken up and is coming over."

In a burst of irascibility, Martha said, "Great. With all three of us here, the nut job who's stalking us will have one-stop shopping for lemmings. How do we know he didn't kill Devry?"

"Martha! Piers didn't kill Devry and you're being insensitive. No nut job will be coming here, not with that security dog of yours." Helen pointed at Amos who'd rolled over and was sleeping with all four legs in the air and snoring contentedly.

"I am being extremely sensitive, Helen. Sensitive to the reality that we need to find out who wants us dead. What if Fancy Pants tells the wrong person where he's off to? Then they come over here, kill us all and leave our children and pets orphans," cried a high-tempered and overly-tired Martha.

"Okay, okay. You need some rest." Helen tried to soothe Martha while wrestling her out of her chair and nudging her up the stairs. "Take Gus and Amos and go upstairs and have a nap. I'll wait for Piers. Don't worry about anything."

"I'm locking my door and I've got a big club with a sharp nail in it that I keep by my bed. If anyone tries to get into my room, I swear I'll let them have it," Martha threatened from the landing.

"Yeah, yeah. Sounds good. You do that. Thought you knew how to kill with your bare hands. Shouldn't need a bat with a nail. Now go to bed!" Helen yelled back up the stairs.

As Helen walked down the hall into Martha's kitchen, she asked herself, "Why do I feel like I've dropped into that crazy, old movie we were watching? I'm playing Clouseau to her Dreyfus."

She checked her appearance in the toaster and, finding it tidy and acceptable, began boiling water for a private tea for two.

Chapter 30

Prior to the murder investigation, Johns had known of Piers Cousins but had never met him, and thought of him as just another wealthy-type.

"So, tell me about why you came here today, Mr. Cousins?" Johns asked in a nonchalant manner, hoping to put Cousins at ease.

Piers shrugged his shoulders and fiddled with a pen. "I left the hospital with intentions to go home and..."

Johns waited, giving him some time. Cousins might still be in a bit of shock.

"Yes?"

"I thought maybe Louis was Sir Carstons' killer and I wanted to offer him my help."

Johns sat for a few moments quietly considering Cousins.

"Really? What sort of help would you offer to Mr. Devry?"

"I thought I could help with the solicitor's fees. Louis was my friend and we'd known each other since childhood. After his visit to the hospital and knowing how Sir Carstons was blackmailing him..."

"Blackmail? That is news. Please enlighten me." Johns' interest had been tweaked.

"Carstons had something on Louis about his last job at Harvard. Martha, Helen and I saw the security videos. It appeared that Louis was very angry with Carstons the day Carstons was killed. I think there was more to the story and maybe Louis was holding something back."

"Like what?"

"I don't know. Maybe he never forgave Carstons' terrible treatment of Emilia."

"He mentioned when I interviewed him, he'd loved an Emilia. What did you know about the woman?"

"Well…" again a lengthy hesitation. "Chief Inspector, Emilia Carstons and I were involved in a relationship when she died in childbirth. I believe the child she was mine and I've worked for years to get custody of him."

Johns kept his face as stoic as possible. He always got a tingle in his chest when the net started to close. "What makes you think the child is yours, Mr. Cousins?"

"We were lovers. She cut off contact with me right after she knew she was pregnant. I think she feared Sir Carstons and wanted a divorce but he refused. She died wanting to be free of him. Chief, if anyone wanted Carstons dead all these years, it was me." Cousins looked the Chief directly in the eye.

"Gee, Mr. Cousins, are you trying to make it easy on me? Why shouldn't I take you in right now?"

"I didn't kill him," Piers said flatly.

The two men stared at each other long enough to smell the other's solidness. On Johns' part, he didn't have a shred of evidence against Cousins yet. No fingerprints, nothing. The taxi cab driver said he brought Cousins from the hospital. The hospital gave a release time for Cousins. Johns had nothing.

"Mr. Cousins, thank you for your help. I am sorry about Mr. Devry. Where are you planning to go now?"

"To Flower Pot Cottage. I'm going to check on Helen and Martha."

Johns gave Cousins a penetrating look. He immediately became tense. All his instincts were on alert. He decided to buy some insurance.

"Don't tell Mrs. Ryes and Mrs. Littleword because I don't want them to be nervous, but we've had a constant police watch on them and the cottage. Safest place for them. We don't want anything happening to them, do we?" He stared at Cousins coldly.

Piers smiled. "We must both rise to the occasion then, Chief Inspector. I shall make sure and stay with them tonight. To keep them safe, of course."

Johns might have punched Cousins if it hadn't been for his sergeant's timely arrival with a request to come talk with the medical examiner.

The two men exchanged looks of restrained tension and then, like two dogs who didn't want to be the first to walk away, they both turned their shoulders at angles and moved off in different directions, Johns to watch a man be zipped into a black bag and Cousins to drink tea at Flower Pot Cottage.

Scene Break

It was nine p.m. when Johns wrapped up his work at Devry's cottage. He was exhausted. In the last two days, he'd slept little and the lack of sleep was wearing him down. Phoning Constable Waters, he told her he was going home and that she should't disturb him unless aliens landed in Marsden-Lacey. She promised to let the others know and wished him a quiet evening free of Klingons.

Turning in through the gate to his home, he pulled up to the front door, turned off the car's motor and slumped into his seat. Looking back over the last few days, it seemed as if some kind of cosmic tap had been turned and all Hell had broken loose.

As he pondered the current barrage of murder and mayhem, he couldn't help coming back to the notion that it had all begun with the devilish redhead's assault on poor Sam Berry in the High Street. That woman was the definition of difficult.

He hoped she could hold her own with Cousins. A smile broke around the corners of his mouth as he imagined the havoc that woman could wreak if given ample opportunity. Maybe he should have warned Cousins instead of threatening him earlier. Johns watched the moon emerge from a cloud in the black nighttime sky and thought to himself how Mrs. Littleword was a very attractive woman. The image of her shooting perfume into her cleavage and the audacity of her taking a swig from his beer bottle, made him aware of a sudden need to see her again. With a shake of his head to free it of redheads and crime, he got out of the car.

The Johns family had always been civil servants of one kind or another. They started out as bailiffs in the Hundred Courts in the seventeenth century but as times changed, they transitioned into the professions of police work and military service.

The family house had been home to one branch of the family or another for over two hundred and thirty years. Always a working farm up until sixty years ago, it was Johns' grandfather who came back from World War II a Lieutenant Colonel and chose to stay in the military instead of farming. From that point on, the family leased out their land but continued living in the old house.

The front door to the stone farmhouse was unlocked and the light was on down the low-ceilinged hall. Johns heard the radio playing Grieg's "In the Hall of the Mountain King" while he walked to the back of the house.

Coming into the expansive, newly-renovated kitchen/living room, Johns saw the familiar form of his mother ensconced in the ratty winged-back chair near the always warm Aga stove.

"Hi, Mum." He lifted the lid on a steaming pot of beef stew and breathed in the tantalizing smell.

"Oh come now, Merriam, you'd better get a bowl and have a bite to eat. Besides, I've got something interesting to tell you."

Polly Johns was an extremely good-looking widow of sixty-five. Her beautiful snow-white hair was cut in a fashionable short style and with a flair for dressing herself in simple, elegant clothes, she was truly a fine figure of a woman.

Making homemade beer which she brewed in a converted section of the old family barn was her passion. Over the last ten years, Polly's profit from her brewing skills allowed her to renovate the old house, giving it a second lease on life.

Johns filled his brown pottery bowl with steaming hot stew and cut off a good-sized piece of his mother's homemade potato bread. Opening one of her own pale ales, Polly poured it into a chilled mug and set it before her son.

For a few minutes all he did was eat, quietly savoring each bite. Mother and son sat together in peaceful silence while Polly watched with contentment as Johns ate what she'd made especially for him.

Johns broke the spell of domestic bliss. "Better tell me the hot gossip from Harriet's, Mum. Let me guess. The crew at Harriet's shop and the Traveller's Inn have a raving maniac running loose on our streets and they're about to have my badge recalled."

Johns' mother was never so pleased as when her detective inspector son was clueless and completely off the mark in his assumptions. It tickled her Irish sense of humor.

"No, dear, quite the opposite. You know how much they love you. It was only yesterday that Mrs. White, your first grade teacher, stopped me in the market and told me how proud she was of you. Even if you struggled with mathematics she said, you'd always been such a brilliant boy and dedicated to your school work."

Johns raised his eyebrows and shook his head in a gesture of bemusement. "So that's the news? Mrs. White remembers my academic challenges?"

"Merriam, be patient and let me tell you." She refilled his bowl with stew and gave him a flick on the back of his head to bring his attitude back in line with where she thought it should be. "Do you remember how Angus Ruskin had that wife for two years and then she disappeared? Everyone thought Angus sent her away to the sanitarium because she was always walking around the village at night with only her nightdress on and a pair of wellies. We were completely wrong. Actually, she moved to Oxton to get away from Angus who was quite difficult to live with after he'd been drinking all night at the pub. That's why she was often outside, poor thing. He would toss her out into the street. Good for her, for leaving the villain."

She paused in her story to see if he was still listening. "Does that town sound familiar to you?"

158

"Town? Uh, Oxton you mean? Yes, that's where Devry said he went to visit his stepmother. Why would you know anything at all about the Oxton connection?" Johns asked with a refreshed alertness in his voice.

"Well, you see that's it. You'll never guess who walked into Harriet's today and I might say looked extremely fit and put together?"

"Angus Ruskin's wife? I hope she has a name."

Polly, with a gleam in her eye like a mongoose who's cornered her prey, hesitated in order to build up the tension and expectation of her audience.

"Mum, get to it. You know this kind of thing makes me crazy. What was Ruskin's wife doing in town?"

"Marsha is her name and she came to town because she brought Devry's stepmother to see him."

"Yesterday?" Johns couldn't believe the timing of Devry's stepmother's visit.

"Thought you would like to know. I'm off to bed but if you would like to know one more thing, I will need a kiss on the cheek before I tell you."

Johns sighed resignedly at the motherly blackmail but knew better than to begrudge Polly her winnings. She was likely to pull his ear, or worse—stop cooking for a fortnight.

Proffering her cheek so Johns could tenderly give her a kiss, she resumed her tale.

"Martha Ruskin and the woman checked out of The Traveller's Inn this morning according to Neil who manages the desk." Polly then patted her son's bristly head. "Well, good night, Merriam. I love you. Sleep well."

Johns watched his mother climb the back stairs and heard her door shut. Putting his bowl in the sink and turning off the lights, he followed her up the stairs and to his own room. For tonight, rest was all he could think of, but tomorrow he would be making a much needed visit to Oxton.

Scene Break

As the moon rose high in the nighttime sky, the town of Marsden-Lacey closed its shutters, locked its doors and took comfort in the simple pleasures of bed and silence. Helen and Martha, slept so deeply that Helen didn't even notice she had a cat curled up next to her head. Piers told the girls he would sleep on the couch at Flower Pot to give them peace of mind.

Not all the inhabitants slept peacefully though. Some hatched a plan to return a treasure, some fretted about their loved ones and one in particular plotted murder. As to this last person it must be added that they did it for love, but then many horrors have been credited to the power of that emotion.

Chapter 31

Satisfied his appearance would equal or better Cary Grant's jewel thief character in "To Catch a Thief," Perigrine smiled at his sleek, black-garbed silhouette in the mirror. He knew it was best to always dress appropriately for any occasion and who better to emulate in this instance than a successful cat thief and one who was dastardly good-looking and debonair much like himself.

With his ensemble in place, it was time to put on the knapsack. Unfortunately for Perigrine, the backpack was bright yellow, but it fit well to his back and was the only thing he could find to carry the manuscript in successfully. Doing a few hops around the room, first on two legs and then on one foot each, he concluded the pack wouldn't slosh around if his movements where exaggerated.

Many years ago, Perigrine and Alistair were preparing to do a job in Austria and decided to learn to ski while they were there. They found to their surprise, they were excellent skiers, so they invested in all the equipment necessary to ski well and look good while doing so. Since then, they'd given up skiing, but tonight Perigrine managed to find one of their old black, knitted face mask to hide his face in case anyone should see him en route to the Constabulary.

Donning the ski mask, he took stock of himself again in the mirror and did a few more hops to make sure of his spryness for the night's adventure. The yellow and black mask with his entirely black body and the yellow backpack made Perigrine resemble a stretched-out skinny bee. The hopping gave the impression the bee was having difficulty with its takeoff.

Finally, he checked the rubber soles of his shoes by taking a run at the opposite side of the room to see if they had grip. They had grip. He did a nice landing into a heap of Comstock's never-used dog beds.

Pleased to see he still had the flexibility of body and quickness of mind to be agile, he hoped he was also still quick-witted in tight situations. The anticipation of the night ahead filled him with excitement. It had been a long time since he'd felt so alive. He loved the thrill of the heist. This time though, he was on the side of the law which gave a certain honor and righteousness to his night's endeavors.

Picking up the manuscript, he gave it one more look. He was taking on the dangerous task of returning what Alistair had lifted. If he was caught, he would probably be put back in jail. This in itself was a horrifying thought, but it would be the loss of faith from his new village friends that would be the hardest thing for him to accept. He and Alistair had made a new life here and the people of Marsden-Lacey had become like an adopted family.

So the pressure was on: save Ally from being arrested while not being arrested himself. He put the manuscript in the knapsack and did one more set of hops.

Alistair, for his part, was sleeping comfortably in the other room with Comstock tucked into his arm. He had absolutely no idea what P. was up to. Perigrine thought it best to keep it that way for now. Only Comstock lifted his head and blinked his small black eyes when P. peeked in on them. The dog gave a great yawn and let his head fall back on Alistair's arm.

It was shortly after midnight when Perigrine gingerly let himself out the back door of their house. Since the pub closed early during the week, most of the villagers should be at home. He put on his leather driving gloves and thanked God it wasn't raining as he slipped around to the side of the Constabulary.

Only the front reception room lights were on, meaning the two constables on the night shift, Michael and Thomas, were tending the desk. They always kept the police radio going during the night and its droning, Perigrine hoped, would cover the sound of his entry through one of the windows.

Thomas and Michael loved watching fishing videos about big-game fishermen. They spent their evenings glued to the computer discussing different techniques for catching fish. So, Perigrine's only real difficulty was finding an open window and, of course, not being caught. He intended to put the manuscript back in Johns' office. There it would be safe.

Fortunately for Perigrine, he was familiar with every aspect of the station. For instance, he knew a surveillance system was recently installed thanks to Donna telling him earlier, so he must be careful to avoid being detected by any cameras.

Crawling along between the building and the shrubbery, he gently tugged on each window at ground level. None were open. It seems the Constabulary had learned its lesson. Since Alistair's robbery, the place was on lockdown. Looking for help from above, he saw to his relief a back window on the second floor was slightly ajar. All he needed was a ladder and that was easy since the Constabulary had one they kept up against the outdoor sheds.

A single camera covered this side of the building. It was quickly dealt with by coming up behind it and putting a bag over it. Then with the nerves of a true cat burglar, Perigrine found the ladder and affixed it against the back of the Constabulary directly under the window of choice. He nimbly started to climb, but halfway up, his ascent was arrested by a light being turned on in the room he was heading for. The sounds of two male voices came wafting out through the slender opening of the window.

"Mike, you aren't keeping your wrist locked. Even if you bring it back to a ten o'clock position, you always keep your wrist firm," Thomas, the other constable, was saying.

With nerves of steel, Perigrine continued his climb and with remarkable composure lifted his head above the window's sill to look inside. There was Thomas and Michael practicing fly rod casts in the exercise room.

"They could be there for hours," P. thought, so he descended back to the ground and decided to take the Police Station by storm: through the front door.

He worked his way around to the front of the building, careful to avoid camera angles and for at least fifteen minutes watched the reception area. There were two cameras covering the front but no movement of any kind inside the building.

Perigrine worked his way along the side of the building using the different voluminous bushes for cover. He'd barely secreted himself in a massive hydrangea bush when an alarm began to ring right above his head. Perigrine's heart felt like it had lept into his throat as his entire frame went rigid. Perigrine the Cat was as still as a statue.

Michael was yelling something as Thomas' feet thundered down the wooden stairs inside. Somehow Perigrine's body acted on its own volition. He leaped back along the way he'd come and once under the complete shield of darkness, ran blindly toward the back of the building again. It was his only chance of escape. Lights sprang up in the yard and Perigrine plastered himself against a dark section of wall, his chest heaving from exertion and excitement. Looking around wildly, he saw a young man dart down the bike path across the main street.

Peregrine wasn't sure what was going on but he could hear voices coming toward him. The only route open was into the back yard where the police vehicles were parked. He could hear men shouting and the alarm seemed to grow louder than ever, so P. did the only thing he could do: he ran for one of the squad cars praying it would be unlocked. Unfortunately for P., the gods were bored tonight and decided to have even more fun with him.

The first car door he fiddled with was the back one to a police vehicle. It opened. Jumping into the backseat, he pulled the door closed, finding himself in a cage used to transport prisoners. With horror, Perigrine quickly realized that neither of the back doors could be opened except from the outside. He frantically tried the doors to no avail. Locked in like a cat in a cage, Perigrine would have kicked himself but he didn't have the room.

As he squashed himself on the back floorboard of the squad car, he considered how nice it would be to thrash Alistair and made a promise to never watch another Cary Grant film for the

164

rest of his life. It was sometime immediately after this last thought, he heard Michael's and Thomas' voices growing louder as they approached the car. It was too late to do anything but sit quietly in the floorboard, do a sign of the cross and pray.

Scene Break

"Who's escaped?" Johns mumbled half-asleep into the phone. "Sam? Sam Berry? I'm going to kill him! Yes, I'll be there. Give me twenty minutes. Wait. I think it would be better if you came and got me. Had some to drink before bed. Be here in ten."

The young constable, Michael, who'd only moments before had been practicing his fly rod casting, sounded the alarm and hurriedly ran out to the car park to go fetch Johns. He jumped into the first vehicle he came to. It happened to be the first one Perigrine came to as well, so unbeknownst to Michael, there was a stowaway hiding less than six inches behind him.

Michael pressed the gas and tore out of the car park forcing the vehicle to race down the back lanes of Marsden-Lacey. With lights flashing and heart beating, Perigrine was being hurled toward his fate while forcibly crunching himself as low as possible in the backseat's floorboard. All too soon, the car came to an abrupt stop outside DCI Johns' house. Once Michael extricated himself from the vehicle and ran up to the door, P. tried frantically to work the door latch. It was a pointless exercise.

Soon, Johns and Michael both returned to the car and jumped in once more. Perigrine reassumed his crouched position behind the front seat. The car sped away into the night.

The ride only lasted another five minutes. With an abrupt stop, both policemen jumped out of the car and banged on a door yelling, "Sam!"

The house door opened and after some brief conversation, it slammed shut and the night went quiet.

Perigrine peeked over the front seat and saw no one in sight. They were all inside. Taking advantage of what little time he probably had, he began squeezing himself through the tiny enclosure between the front and back seat. It took some doing, but Perigrine managed to work himself like a piece of dough through the opening and onto the front seat.

Once through the opening, he lay flat on the front seat and pushed open the passenger door sliding from the seat to the ground. Using the door as a screen, he took off the knapsack, opened it and laid the manuscript on the front seat, wiping it one last time to remove any prints. It hadn't been the plan to return the manuscript in this way, but without a doubt, Johns would have it back and be no more the wiser regarding who stole it.

Perigrine waited and watched before taking a deep breath then sprinting across to the dark grove of trees on the side of the road. There he hid himself behind a tree and waited.

Soon Johns, Michael, and another young man came out of the house. Johns had the young one by the back of his collar making him walk on his tiptoes.

Letting him drop, Johns began to chastise him. "Sam, you've got to quit breaking out of jail especially late at night."

"She's gonna marry another man, Chief. I will not stand for it," Sam said more at an upper story window than to Johns.

"Well, if you would quit running around mugging women and breaking out of jail, she might look on you more favorably," Johns said in an exasperated tone. "I'm done with you, Sam. You're going HM Prison Wetherby."

"Aw, Chief, please don't," Sam begged. "I promise not to run again. Don't take me away from my Penny."

"You'd better not ever get me out of bed again, Sam, or I'll thrash you myself. Do you understand me?" Johns shook the kid again by the back of his collar.

"I do. I do. I'll be the soul of goodness, I will," Sam promised, sounding more like a rattled doll than an ardent, misguided lover.

"Good. Get in." Johns dropped him again and shoved him toward the back door of the car.

"Good night, Penny!" Sam yelled. "Don't marry that clod, Jeffrey. I'll be out soon and I'll be back to marry you!"

"Come on Casanova, get in the car." Johns pushed the kid into the back seat.

Michael was in the driver's seat and when Johns finally got in, Michael flopped the manuscript into his lap with a mischievous smile on his face. "Looks like someone left you a present, Chief."

"What the Hell?" Johns asked staring stupefied at the object in his lap. "What the bloody Hell is it doing out here? Sam, look at this. Do you know anything at all about it?"

"Nah," Sam said indifferently. He continued sending wistful looks up at the second floor of the house.

"Michael, did you see anything   anyone?"

"Sir, I didn't see anything. Inside with you of course the whole time."

"Well, I'll be…I'll be."

Meanwhile, Perigrine was using the GPS on his phone to find his way back home. He had a pretty good walk ahead of him, but his step was light with the pleasant knowledge that he'd performed a great deed. His thirst for adventure was satiated. Well, at least for the time being.

Chapter 32

Morning dawned in Marsden-Lacey and it was lovely and crisp. The summer was getting on. Dew made the grass and hedges glisten. Birds sang their songs and did their dances in appreciation of the plentitude of mother nature.

Humans emerged from their homes in different forms of attire. Some were dressed more professionally than others. Milkman, publican, solicitor, teacher, tradesman and so on. But it was Martha in her flannel valentine pajamas, matching fluffy, red robe and Garfield house shoes tending to her overgrown garden with a cup of coffee in her hand, that brought a smile to the occasional passerby's face.

"You want some breakfast, Martha?" Helen called out the kitchen window.

Happily dead-heading a petunia plant, Martha looked up and called back, "I'm starving. Look in the refrigerator. You'll find all sorts of bacon, sausages, potatoes and eggs. I'll come in to help."

She watched a wide beam canal boat glide quietly along the canal as the mist rose over the water creating a mystical feeling. The boat had a little chimney stack puffing out clouds of smoke hinting at a warm, cozy interior cabin. A man guiding the boat tipped his hat to Martha and smiled. She in turn gave him a bright wave and thought about what he would see today and how by tonight he would have his boat moored in a new village or maybe out in the lovely English countryside. Her heart fill with pleasure as she thought about how much she loved her waterside home.

Amos' bark at her doorstep meant Martha should come inside and give the pint-sized dog a bit of bacon. The delicious aroma filled the air with the best breakfast smell in the world and Amos was terribly insistent to receive her fair share any time bacon was cooked in the house. Kate, Martha's daughter, spoiled Amos rotten when she was home, treating her from Kate's own plate with any goody the little dog might savor.

"Oh, hi handsome," Martha said to Piers as she came into the kitchen. "Hope you slept comfortably last night."

Helen rolled her eyes at Martha's impersonation of Mae West.

"Slept like a baby." Piers rubbed Amos between her ears. "Didn't have a nurse poking me or waking me up to take my vitals. Could have done without that dog of yours jumping on me at three o'clock in the morning though."

Martha buttered the toast to put in the oven. "She wanted you to take her outside. Should we put sugar and cinnamon on these?" She dug in the cabinet and found the cinnamon and handed it to Helen then picked up a piece of bacon and chewed on it.

"I took her out and she sniffed at every bush while my bare feet were freezing."

Helen brought the cinnamon to the table and plunked it down on the table indicating Martha could do the toast. "Let's do. I haven't had cinnamon toast since I was a child. I'll let you do the honors." She playfully poked at Martha's shoulder to get her to start working.

"Are you both Southerners?" Piers asked.

The girls looked at each other and chuckled.

"What gave us away? The accent or the love of bacon? You'll have to come over sometime for my red beans and rice, Piers. It'll put some meat on your bones," Martha said with a twinkle in her eyes.

He chuckled and asked Helen, "What about you Mrs. Ryes? Are you going to offer me a truly southern meal sometime?"

Helen put a heaping plate of bacon, toast, eggs and grits in front of him. The flirtatious grin he gave her made her toes wiggle. In return she gave him a sweet smile and said in her best Scarlet O'Hara voice, "Why Mr. Cousins, I just did. When was the last time you had real grits like that?"

"Is that what they're called?" He took a bite. "Mmm. These are incredible. I want Mrs. Thyme to learn to make this dish." He mixed the eggs together with the grits.

Helen put a plate down in front of Martha who happily picked up the toast and began pulling off the crust.

"Amos, you're deserving of a special treat," Helen said while she turned more bacon in the skillet. "She barks at every person who comes within twenty feet of this house."

To underscore her affection for the great protector of hearth and home, she gave Amos an entire piece of bacon.

Thunderstruck as a dog can be at the enormity of the woman's recognition by bacon, Amos for a brief second wasn't sure if she should accept the ultimate dog gift. Her true canine nature kicked in and not taking any chances on the whims of humans, she clamped down on the slice of bacon which was almost as long as she was and hustled out of the room to parts unknown.

"Great, now she'll wake me up in the middle of the night to reheat it. Spoiled dog." Martha laughed.

"Not me. I'm going home. I miss the old heap and want to see what damage has been done since I've been incapacitated," Piers said. "What are you doing today?"

His question made Martha realize she hadn't been to work for two days. Her immediate reaction was short of panic. "Helen, if I don't get to work I'm not going to have a job anymore."

She looked down at her plate and continued, "It's funny, though, how I still have my appetite. Darn thing never goes away."

Helen and Piers watched Martha swirl her scrambled eggs around on her plate.

Impulsively, Martha said, "What if I come to work for you, Helen? I excel at research and I bet you could train me to be an excellent assistant. Normally, I'm very conscientious."

Helen laid down her spatula and gave her new friend a penetrating look. "Would you, Martha? I would love it if you came to work with me. Don't offer though unless you really mean it. I think we would make a great team."

Martha flushed pink and for a moment was completely without words. She'd spoken her thoughts without thinking. Lately, the paralegal job she went to everyday felt like being on a treadmill. The last couple of days made her feel alive again. Helen's warmth, true joy at having her for a work mate, and the fact they shared a common background, made Martha start to tear up.

"I'll do it if you'll have me," Martha said starting to cry. "Helen, if you are serious, I would love to try something new. Thank you." She got up and gave Helen a big hug.

They took stock of each other. One in a strange-looking red robe and the other in pajamas with ice-cream cones all over them (an old pair of Kate's), they laughed through their happy tears.

"Good." Piers dabbed at the corners of his mouth with a napkin. "Now that you are both settled, I have a job for you. I need my entire library gone over and when you girls can fit me in, I would be glad to have your expert opinions on my collection."

Once Helen and Martha were done doing their happy hopping and hugging each other, they gave Piers a big kiss on both his cheeks which made the Englishman blush. He wasn't exactly accustomed to high emotional American female outbursts.

"May we come by this afternoon, Mr. Cousins, to do a small assessment of your collection?" Helen asked in a put-on professional tone.

"Delighted to have you. How about three, tea time?" Piers said in his best Etonian accent.

"We'll be there," Martha and Helen said in perfect unison.

Chapter 33

Chief Johns was on his way to Oxton to visit with Devry's stepmother. The events of the previous evening kept nagging at him. He couldn't unravel why anyone living along last night's road would be remotely interested in an old manuscript. Most people living in the area wouldn't cross the road to visit the library let alone crawl into the police station to steal a book.

The surveillance videos from the police station last night showed a few prowlers around the place. Two teenagers on bikes using the back lot to access the walking path, someone stumbling around in the bushes, probably a drunk looking for a place to relieve himself, and Sam making a break for it down the alley. Nothing unexpected. So, it must mean someone followed their police vehicle, waited until they were inside and put the manuscript in the car.

He thought on it for a while longer finally giving it up. He would check it off his list for the time being. The trip to Oxton would take at least an hour with traffic. He needed the time to focus on the Carstons case.

The report was back on Devry's death and the details wouldn't be released to the public yet. He needed to first talk with Devry's stepmother, but it was obvious Devry was murdered and someone wanted his death to look like a suicide.

There were too many factors pointing to this. Devry's mobile phone calendar showed he'd a vacation planned for Majorca in only two weeks. Depressed people don't usually kill themselves before going to a beautiful, exotic locale.

The alarm on Devry's mobile was set for eleven a.m. which meant he intended to be at the station to meet Johns regarding the manuscript. People who commit suicide don't set alarms for later in their day and then drink an entire bottle of booze and a massive dose of Klonopin.

But the best reason for Devry not killing himself came from hard evidence. Most of the medicine he'd swallowed was in his stomach but two pills were found still in his mouth. People who want to kill themselves swallow all their pills.

The medicine Devry swallowed would have taken time to stop his respiration, plenty of time for him to swallow every pill. The autopsy found Scotch in his mouth and his stomach. Someone shoved those pills into his mouth and followed it with Scotch. But, because Devry was asleep when it was administered, he hadn't swallowed everything.

No glass by his bed. No glass in the sink either. Another mistake by the murderer. Someone washed the glass to get rid of their fingerprints. This meant the murderer hadn't visited expecting to kill Devry and maybe couldn't pass up the golden opportunity when it was presented. Someone wanted it to look like a suicide.

The pills found in Devry's stomach and mouth were for anxiety. Devry's doctor had weighed in on the death as well. According to the doctor, in the last three months, Devry had suffered from severe anxiety attacks. New job, new country, but mostly because of something weighing on his mind he wouldn't discuss with the doctor.

Whoever killed Devry found an opportune moment and made the most of it. There wasn't a sign of a struggle in his cottage and no prints were found anywhere. Devry looked as peaceful as a baby when Johns saw him. No suffering, no pain; either mental or physical. Only peace.

Were the two murders connected? Why would Carstons' killer want Devry dead, too? And Johns couldn't forget the attempt on Cousins life. The three men shared two things in common. One was The Grange and the other was a woman. Money, jealousy, and power: three reasons to kill.

As for Cousins, he definitely wanted Sir Carstons out of the way because of the ongoing financial problems Carstons was causing for The Grange's Board. However, he also wanted custody of his love child with Carstons' wife which the man had consistently blocked.

The car traveled effortlessly along the motorway. Traffic was flowing nicely allowing Johns to maintain an easy rhythm to both his driving and his musing on the case.

Piers Cousins was still alive. He would be a nice bet in Johns' opinion to be the killer. The Chief Detective Inspector smiled at the pleasant thought of arresting Cousins for the murders. His opinion of Cousins was at a low since their conversation yesterday and sometimes Johns' humanness slipped through letting him, like anyone else, indulge in his own happy fantasies.

But it wasn't to last for long, as he continued the mental puzzle solving game of grouping clues with times and locations of each person involved in the case, he was forced to admit that Cousins' alibis for both murders was rock solid. This brought a return of the habitual, earlier scowl to his face. He tried to make the pieces fit with one last effort. What if Cousins had someone make a fake attempt on his life to throw the police off his trail? Maybe, but not likely. Taking a bullet in the middle of a dance floor while dancing was way too unpredictable. Johns shifted mental gears.

Carstons, Cousins and Devry shared the love of a woman or maybe they loved her but she didn't return the feeling. What about this Emilia? How many lovers had she?

Also, there was the card with Cousins' name found on the rock door stop used to kill Carstons. If Cousins had Sir Carstons killed, he wouldn't have let his name be literally on the murder weapon.

Johns' musings came to an abrupt end as he entered the outskirts of Oxton. He easily found the address of Devry's stepmother. She lived in a small retirement housing village.

The name on her house read "Rose Bungalow" and with a look around to the other small domiciles, he realized each was named after an English flower. He pulled the car along the curb, got out and went to the door to ring the bell.

It took some time, but finally a small white-haired woman came to the door and without taking the chain from the latch asked in a feeble voice, "Yes?"

"Mrs. Devry?"

"Yes, I'm Carissa Devry."

I'm Chief Detective Inspector Johns from the Marsden-Lacey Police Department." He showed her his badge. "May I have a moment of your time?"

The diminutive woman gave him a hard look. "One moment, please. I will go get my daughter."

She shut the door completely. He grimaced. You never knew at this point if you would have to ring again.

Soon a middle-aged, pleasant-looking woman with light brown hair opened the door. "How may we help you?"

Again, Johns showed his badge and she gave it a cursory glance.

"I am Chief Detective Inspector Johns with the Marsden-Lacey Police Department. May I come in and talk with you and your mother? It's regarding her stepson, Louis Devry."

"Yes, of course. Please come in. My name is Isabelle Benton. Mum will be in the back of the house. It's a nice sunny room so she likes to sit there during the day."

Isabelle Benton showed Johns into the room. The elderly Carissa motioned for him to join her and said, "Dear, would you please bring us some coffee? You would like something warm to drink, Inspector? I think fall is in the air. It's a bit chilly."

"Yes, Ma'am. That would be nice."

"I'll be right back, Mum."

Once the younger woman left the room, Mrs. Devry, wrapped in a fuzzy shawl, looked up and gave Johns a shy smile. "I don't have many visitors from where my son lives. Why have you come such a long way today, Inspector?"

There, briefly, a tiny muscle spasm at the corner of her eye told him she sensed something wrong with his visit. She pulled the shawl tighter around her shoulders trying to ward off the creeping coldness he'd brought into the room. Johns inwardly steeled himself for the coming conversation.

Isabelle returned and sat down by her mother. She gave Johns a concerned look. "Why have you come here, Chief Inspector?"

There wasn't an easy way to say it. With a tight hold on his heart, he grimaced and jumped into the unpleasant truth. "I am sorry to be the one to bring this news to you…"

Mrs. Devry held up her small, white hand to stop him. She turned her head to the window and Johns could see the tremors begin in her frail, bird-like body. Tears filled her eyes and began to roll down the delicate paper-like skin of her white cheeks.

"Oh, Mother," the younger woman said reaching out to take the still upheld hand into her own. She gave Johns a pleading, unsure look. "It's okay, Mum," she said, trying to reassure them both.

This was the absolute worst part of Johns' job. He told them of Louis' death and sat with them for at least thirty minutes with his elbows resting on his knees and his hands clasped waiting for them to be ready for the rest of his story.

At one point the water begin to boil so he went into the kitchen, made tea and brought it out to them. Handing the tissues as needed, Johns poured them each a cup. Finally, the shock rolled back briefly from them like a wave returns back into the deep of the sea only to return again sometimes with even more force and passion.

"How did he die?" Isabelle asked.

Johns' eyes flitted from one woman's face to the other. Not sure how much he should attempt considering the elderly lady's health, he said, "To be fair to you both, it's still a matter of investigation. He passed away yesterday around midday."

"Isabelle. I'd just been there." Mrs. Devry said. "Oh, my God, Isa, I'd just been there. Oh, dear, dear Louis."

176

The tiny woman began to cry again and tried to lift herself from her chair. Her daughter, with a look of concern quickly escalating to fear due to her mother's reaction, helped Mrs. Devry out of her chair. She looked at Johns like he was a murderer.

"Help me get her to her room, please. She should lie down."

Johns practically carried Mrs. Devry to her bedroom and while her daughter was quieting her down, he sat in the cheery sunroom and drank his tea. Soon Isabelle returned and sat on the sofa looking pale and tired.

She stared out the window. "Louis was fine when mum left yesterday. He was looking forward to his upcoming trip to Majorca. How did he die so suddenly? Was it a heart attack?"

"Ms. Benton, it's too premature for us to know exactly how your brother died. I wanted to come today to tell your mother and to ask her a few questions."

He hurried on before she could state the obvious. "Was your mother's visit purely for pleasure? Mr. Devry mentioned before to me during an interview that she'd been ill and he came to stay with her last week."

"Well, yes, and no. A friend of my mother's from church was going to Marsden-Lacey and invited mother. Mother was feeling stronger and wanted to surprise Louis."

"Ms. Benton," he began.

"It's Mrs. Benton. So you know." She smiled weakly.

"Mrs. Benton, was your brother depressed or anxious about anything in the last couple of months?"

She hesitated. Johns waited.

"Louis was distracted but we knew he was under a great deal of pressure to succeed at this new post. You see, Louis lost his last job at Harvard for some type of indiscretion. He wouldn't talk about it. Piers wanted him for the position at The Grange in Marsden-Lacey and mother was so happy to have him back here."

"Do you know anything at all about the indiscretion?"

"We hoped it was to do with a woman." Another weak smile. "He was so close-mouthed about it. Wouldn't tell us a thing."

"Why did you hope it was to do with a woman?"

"Louis was the sweetest man alive. He never got over that silly woman, Emilia. You know they had this great love affair when they were younger but she ran off to Switzerland. He only saw her one other time about six or seven years ago. She married a rich man so Louis gave up on it and went back to his job in America."

"Went back to his job? What do you mean?"

Again, she held something back and told him the glossy version. "Yes, he went back to his job at Harvard. He came here for a visit and saw Emilia. He never really got over her."

"Did you know she died?"

"Yes, mother told me. We were both relieved he was coming home finally and wouldn't have that constant heartache so close by."

Johns stood up to go. "When was the last time you saw your brother?"

"He was here last week. Friday it was. Louis had received a telephone call asking him to come see mother. When he got here, mother and I, were both surprised to see him. No one here had called him."

"Thank you, Mrs. Benton. I may have other questions later. You'll be contacted today about the arrangements. Please accept my sympathy."

"Before you go, Chief Inspector, was Louis' death unnatural?" she asked him point blank.

"Yes, Mrs. Benton, I believe it was. We're treating it as a homicide and would appreciate your discretion until we have more information."

She bit her upper lip and stood up. "I'll be right back." She motioned for him to wait.

A few minutes passed and she returned handing him a letter. He saw it was from an attorney in Hartford, Connecticut. It stated that Emilia Carstons requested that upon her death, Louis Devry should be informed they shared a child.

Johns looked dumbstruck. He said, "This is dated two weeks ago. Emilia Carstons has been dead for years. Why all of a sudden did he receive this letter?"

"Her will was tied up for years and her family is all dead. I know her husband fought to regain rights to her inheritance but the family in Connecticut hated him. They never wanted him to be able to touch her money so the father cut her off when she married him. This would have made Louis rich and a father."

"What did your brother think about being a father?"

"Terrified. To be honest, I think he was numb to the idea. He didn't even respond to the attorney's letter. He couldn't get his bearings because he was obsessed with Emilia. The boy would have to be about six or seven years old now. The child would have been a sad reminder of her."

Johns tried to keep his face unemotional. He never allowed himself to judge other people's motives or actions. That was for the courts. "May I keep this for a while, Mrs. Benton?"

"Of course. Thank you for coming all this way."

Johns left Rose Bungalow with something he hadn't had before: a motive for murder.

Chapter 34

The day was perfect. Rainy, cloudy, and cold. Martha and Helen spent the morning organizing the structure of their new working relationship. Since Helen's divorce, she'd been trying to do the job of three people without a great deal of success.

Martha was a perfect fit. With years of experience managing people, she was organized, detail-oriented and a trifle on the compulsive side. Keeping clients happy, doing research until late into the night, and creating tidy case files made her a favorite among the attorneys she worked for. In her last job she'd become the firm's senior paralegal, which meant she managed the other paralegals to make sure they were following protocol.

The girls felt good about their new venture and with a new client to see about, they were busy. Helen suspected their work at The Grange would be at least a six-month project and a follow-up project at Healy had her considering a potential relocation to Marsden-Lacey. With much to consider and discuss, they chatted happily as they drove to Healy for their meeting with Piers.

The weather was delicious. Both women never regretted staying in England after their mates were gone. Even on days requiring a raincoat and wellies, there was always a warm pub or cottage fire to retreat to. There, one could enjoy a warm scone with clotted cream and a hot cup of strong tea.

On this particular rainy day, they would be enjoying tea at Healy House. Piers promised Mrs. Thyme would make it herself which meant it would be not only beautiful to see but delicious as well. Needless to say, they were excited. Their conversation turned to Helen's and Piers' tête-à-tête the other night while Martha was sleeping.

"I think he's a big flirt, Helen."

"Takes one to know one."

"True. Tread lightly around him. He's used to having women throw themselves at him." Martha shifted the Mini into fourth gear. The Green Bean zipped along between hedgerows and stone walls with the windshield wipers beating out a soft, sleepy tune.

"Don't worry, for the time being, I'm not sure having another man in my life is what I want anyway. He's charming, but," Helen shrugged her shoulders, "he might be too much too soon."

Martha considered Helen's point. Through the sprinkles falling on the windshield, she could see a shepherd and his dog working to corral a flock of sheep down in a pasture. A fine mist hovered right above the valley giving the entire scene a feeling of tranquility and timeless beauty. The landscape made her nostalgic for a simpler time in her own life.

"I was happy in my marriage, but after Martin died I didn't even consider seeking a new relationship. Kate came first and I wanted to raise her. Besides, I loved Martin and he would be a hard act for any man to follow. I understand where you're coming from. No more teasing from me, if you like."

"I like." Helen smiled at Martha. "Besides, if he's a flirt, then I'm going to practice my hand at it. Goodness knows, I deserve to play a bit. Right?"

"Right," Martha said with conviction. "Piers Cousins may be just the medicine you need, Helen. He definitely is putting his money where his interests lay."

The road started to rise over a hill and once at the top, the view stretching out below them was delightful. There in the valley sat Healy with the river running along its left-hand side. They could make out smoke coming from one of the chimneys.

"We're going to have a fire," Martha said with joy. "It's a perfect day for it. Isn't it, Helen?"

"Good thing you like the cold." Helen shivered. "Good thing I brought my big sweater."

In another five minutes they'd brought the car to a gravel-crunching stop right at the front steps of Healy. As they ascended the front stairs, Martha turned to Helen and said with a wink, "Not a bad place to be queen, huh?"

"Nope," Helen answered, "not bad at all."

Scene Break

Johns needed to see Cousins to talk with him about what he learned from Devry's mother. He initially tried calling the house number Cousins gave him, but there wasn't any answer so he left a message. For now, he would stop by the station and pick up one of the constables. They would go together to Healy and wait for Cousins, if they had to.

His phone rang. It was a number he didn't recognize, but he answered it. "Hello?"

"Is this the Chief Inspector?" a woman asked.

"Yes. Who is this?"

"I'm Mr. Cousins' personal secretary. He wanted to let you know he'll be out this afternoon for a business meeting at The Grange. If you'd like to arrange a meeting for tomorrow, I'm to help arrange an appointment."

"I'd like to talk with him today instead of tomorrow," Johns said gruffly.

"Today won't work. After his meeting this afternoon, he'll be going to Leeds to meet with his solicitor. Tomorrow morning is the earliest time available."

Johns sighed irritably. "Fine. How does nine a.m. tomorrow sound?"

"Perfect. We'll see you then. Thank you, Chief Inspector."

Johns hung up. He decided to go directly to The Grange and wait for Cousins. As he maneuvered the car back onto one of Marsden-Lacey's main roads, he thought dryly how lovely it must be to have people managing every little detail of your life like Cousins.

Rain started hitting his windshield.

"Bloody rain," he grumbled. He slowed his speed down only a minuscule amount. He'd every intention of catching Cousins at The Grange.

Scene Break

Constable Waters was tired of Sam's constant whining and requests for his mobile phone. Johns, earlier that day, gave the okay for Donna to let Sam earn opportunities to use his phone by showing good behavior each day. Donna went back to his cell and studied the scraggly young teenager.

"Sam, how old are you?" she asked.

"Seventeen. Why?" he asked sullenly.

"Want some advice about women?"

"Not really. You're probably going to say the same thing as my aunt." He poked the tip of his boots between the spokes of one of the chairs in his cell.

"Stop, messing with the chair," Donna said in her no-nonsense tone which made him pull his toe out of the spokes but then roll his eyes.

"You mugged Martha in the marketplace last week?"

"Yeah, I needed some money. Penny says I'm always broke."

"Thought of getting a job, Sam? There are other ways to get money than mashing women in the street."

"Mashing? I'm the one who got mashed. That crazy woman nearly killed me."

Donna couldn't hold back a smile, thinking of Martha teaching Sam a good lesson. She tried a new approach. "What if I helped you with Penny? She might give you a second look and not marry Jeffrey, if she thought you were making an effort."

Sam sat up on his cot. "Like what?"

"A bath for starters wouldn't hurt and if you know how to use a shaver, you might consider a fresh face. A lot of women enjoy seeing a man's whole face." She smiled brightly while hoping at the same time he wouldn't hear the touch of sarcasm in her voice. "You might be a nice-looking kid somewhere under there."

"Well, I don't know. I like my style."

Donna stifled a guffaw and considered saying something about his "style" but thought better of it. Instead she shifted her tactic. "Want your phone back for an hour?"

The boy bolted off his cot and grabbed the bars in his door. "Now you're talking my language. How do I get the phone?"

"Take a bath, shave your face and put on some decent clothes," she said firmly with a stoic expression.

For ten seconds neither Sam nor Donna broke their eye contact. Eventually, the teenager caved to the mother of two small boys.

With more drama than any fifteen-year-old girl could have managed, Sam flung himself on the bed and said huffily, "Okay. I'll do it."

"Good. I'll get Constable Cross to take you to the showers. I want you to do a smart job on yourself, Sam, otherwise no phone."

More eye rolling and an under-the-breath, "Fine."

It took an hour but what emerged under Constable Cross' tutelage was worthy of an episode of "My Big Juvenile Delinquent Makeover." Sam was actually a handsome young man. Both Donna and Constable Cross told him Penny was missing out if she didn't come around.

All this positive affirmation brightened Sam's mood considerably and he was soon ready for his phone call. Donna took his picture with his phone and Sam sent it via text message to Penny. The two constables kept their fingers crossed and said a few prayers in hope that Penny would respond favorably. While he waited, Sam was allowed to pace the reception area.

A phone rang but it wasn't Sam's. Donna answered it.

It was Johns. "Waters, I'm here at The Grange. I know we're short-staffed but who is on duty besides you?"

184

"Cross."

"Ok, I want you to meet me here at The Grange. I may need to be in more than one place at the same time today."

Sam was still pacing the floor and Donna got an idea. "Chief, could I bring Sam? I want to let him see the other side of the coin so to speak."

"Rehab, huh Waters? Fine. Tell him I chipped him in his sleep so he won't try and escape again. If he does, it's on your head."

"Absolutely. We'll see you in ten minutes." Donna put the phone back into its cradle. "Come on Sam. You're going with me."

"Where to, Boss?" Sam asked.

"We might need lend some support for Chief. Thought you could come along. By the way, Chief says if you try and make a break for it, he'll hunt you down and make you do civic work cleaning the sides of the canal dredger. Understand?"

Sam heaved another dramatic sigh. "Yeah, I understand."

"Let's go then," Donna said and tossed him one of the rain jackets with official Marsden-Lacey Police Department insignia on it. She watched Sam surreptitiously as the young man read the words he'd be wearing across his back. "Put it on," Donna said firmly. "The public need to know if you're working with us."

As he slipped the rain jacket on slowly, she could see by the intent expression on his face, he was experiencing a slight mental shift in his personal perspective. Smiling at being invited to be a part of a team, Sam gave Donna a bright smile.

"I'm ready."

"The Chief is waiting. Let's go then."

Chapter 35

Martha and Helen were met at the door by Sarah, Mrs. Thyme's right-hand girl. All smiles and dimples, she was happy to see them and invited them in, out of the rain.

"Hi, Sarah. We're here to see Mr. Cousins. He invited us to tea and to take a look at his library," Helen said.

"Oh? I'm sorry. He isn't back yet. He went to Leeds today, I think," Sarah said. "Will you please come in, though? I'm sure he'll be back soon. Tea should be ready in about an hour. Would you like to look at the library first?"

Helen and Martha exchanged slightly confused looks.

"Sure," Helen replied.

Sarah asked them to follow her to the library. Following a route, they'd come to know well, through the warm, wood-paneled hall, neither woman attempted a conversation. So much had happened here. The misty weather outside made the elegant room extremely welcoming. A snapping and cheerful fire was laid in the enormous fireplace radiating a comforting warmth. The blaze effectively dissolved any lingering unpleasant memories surrounding the night of the party .

Soon the three women reached the library. As the door swung open to receive them, a tendril of lightening lit up the sky outside of the tall windows facing onto the front drive of Healy.

"If you need me, I'll be in the kitchen helping Senior Agosto. He's leaving soon and he's in a foul temper. Will you be staying for dinner?" Sarah asked.

"We're not exactly sure, but it's doubtful," Martha said with a warm smile for the young girl.

"Okay. Make yourself at home."

Sarah went over to one of the interior walls of the room where bookshelves lined the wall. She pulled a lever built cleverly into the shelf's edge. There was a muffled click and she pushed her way through a panel like one would a door. She smiled at them, and then disappeared, the panel realigning itself like it hadn't been moved in four hundred years.

Alone in the room, Martha turned to Helen and said, "Strange don't you think? Piers not being here, I mean? Did we get the day wrong? Maybe he meant for us to come tomorrow."

"Uh, maybe." Helen said without taking her gaze off the secret door in the bookshelf. "But did you see how Sarah left the room? I want to sneak a peek in there."

"Oh, yeah. I forgot about the secret passage. I saw Piers open the bookshelf on the day of the tennis tournament before the dinner party," Martha said.

Helen walked over to the bookcases and inspected the place where Sarah disappeared. She felt along the inside frame to locate the latch. "This must be a quicker way to the kitchen. Hm…no matter. We better get to work then we can fiddle with secret passages. Piers will show up and probably be all apologies. Might get a yummy dinner out of it."

"Sounds good to me," Martha said. "Where do we start?"

"With the collection records. I want to do an inventory first. We need to make sure everything he thinks is here really is. That'll take us days if not weeks from the look of things. We may have to pull double duty for a while. Is that okay?"

"Are you kidding, Helen? I'm going to have to pinch myself to make sure I'm not dreaming. What a great place to call an office? Let's get to work."

Helen found a shelf which housed nine slender volumes labeled 'Index'. Taking the first one down and delicately going through the pages, she realized how right she was about the time frame. The girls' work was cut out for them.

After about an hour and a half of one person calling out a title and another person locating it, Helen looked up and said, "I'm kind of hungry. How about you?"

"Famished. Let's go down to the kitchen and see if Agosto will let us have a cup of tea and something to nibble on. We can take the back entrance." Martha pointed with a bright, sly smile at the secret door in the bookshelves.

With eyes wide like a child given permission to play hide-and-seek in an old, rambling house, Helen asked, "Do you think we can get it to open?"

"I bet I can do it. Let me see."

Martha walked over to the area followed by Helen. There in the bookshelf they could see the hidden latch and the door where Sarah made her unconventional exit.

"Here's the latch. All we have to do is—"

Like a crash of thunder, a terrific noise ripped through the room. Helen groaned and fell to the floor. Martha reacted instinctively and dropped to a crouch position next to Helen. Luckily they were behind Piers' massive oak desk.

Helen was shot, but the bullet only grazed her upper arm. She blinked at Martha and signaled she was okay. Martha could feel panic starting to rise within her.

Lifting her head in an attempt to see, Martha was forced to duck. Another ripping bang sent papers flying off Piers' desk, filtering down like leaves to rest on top of the girls.

"Help!" they both screamed.

Like a mind-numbing slap to their brains, someone started laughing. It was the laugh from the night they were stalked at The Grange. It was a woman's laugh but it was metallic like it was coming from a machine.

"You know," it said, "there isn't anyone here. They all just left. It's only us girls tonight. I've got a change of plans. No more shooting, if you follow directions. I need you to stand up. We're going for a short walk."

Helen and Martha were in a death grip holding on to each other behind the desk. They looked frantically at one another. Helen shook her head in a frenzied manner to indicate she wasn't about to stand up.

Martha yelled out, "You'll kill us!"

"Dear, if I wanted you dead right now, you'd already be so," the weirdly feminine voice said. "I needed to get your attention. Don't make me come over there or I'll be happy to place my next bullet somewhere to make you more compliant."

Martha considered the offer for a second, but then thought better of it.

"Okay. We'll stand up but give us a moment. Helen is hurt." Martha pointed to the latch on the bookcase shelf.

With a nod to Martha, Helen jumped up and grabbed the latch. Martha pushed the door and they scrambled through as two more gunshots exploded behind them.

Martha slammed the secret door shut and looked for something to jamb it. Someone was working the mechanism from the outside and cursing them in a muffled voice. Helen pointed at an old floorboard propped up against the wall. Martha grabbed it and wedged it between the door and the wall.

Helen asked, "Which way do we go?"

They looked around wildly. There was a passage with stairs going up on the right hand side but there was also one that went behind the stairs and appeared to stay on their present level.

"I don't want to go up. We might not be able to get down again and then out of the house. Let's take the one going behind the stairs," Martha said. "Wait. I want to wrap your arm first."

Martha took off her T-shirt and ripped it along the bottom. She wrapped and tied the make-shift bandage around Helen's arm. Pulling it snug, she knew would put pressure on the wound and slow the bleeding. Quickly she put her shirt back on and they headed along the left-hand route.

As the tight passage wound around corners, the girls kept coming to several potential exits. Martha would try each door handle eagerly only to have their hopes dashed as one after another of the doors were either locked or appeared stuck from years of disuse.

After about five increasingly desperate minutes of walking, they noticed the passage was increasingly filled with bulk food items stacked on both sides. They must be nearing the kitchen.

189

Then the moment they'd been dreading arrived. There was only one more bend before the end of the passage.

"She might be waiting for us," Martha whispered.

Helen didn't move. "Let's go back the other way then."

"What if she's back in there somewhere following us?" Martha pointed down the dark passage behind them.

"Oh dear God. We've got to get to a phone."

Martha tried to get her mind to focus. "Okay. Okay. Okay." She pressed both hands against her forehead. "Let's get down on our knees and I'll peek around again. If it's definitely the kitchen, there's surely an exit. Get down and stay down till I say otherwise."

Martha, with her head low to the floor, edged one eye around the corner. At the end of the passage, she could see a lit corner of the kitchen. No one was in the corridor so she motioned for Helen to follow her and they crawled toward the opening and the feeble kitchen light.

Scene Break

Piers made it the entire way to Leeds from Healy in less than an hour. He pulled up to the front door of his solicitor's office and jumped out of his car, running up the stairs.

He was absolutely ecstatic because his solicitor's paralegal called earlier saying there was a breakthrough in his child custody case. The woman on the phone asked him to come for an appointment that afternoon.

Casey, the firm's receptionist, gave him a big smile when she saw him come through the door. "Hello, Mr. Cousins. How are you today?"

"I'm doing well, Casey, thank you. I hope I made it in time to see Phillip. Drove like a madman to get here," Piers said with a bright smile.

Casey looked slightly confused but she checked her computer and asked Piers to please give her a moment.

Piers sat down.

Phillip Westmorland's voice boomed through the back hallway. Phillip and Piers attended Oxford together. Afterwards, they spent three years traipsing around Australia and California hitting every surfing beach they could find.

"What's this all about, Cousins? Heard you came all the way to Leeds to take me to dinner? You're not my idea of a hot date though," Westmorland said with a laugh.

Piers looked perplexed. "I'll take you to the Ritz, if you want. You deserve it."

Westmorland shrugged egotistically. "Well, I am one hell of a guy."

"Damn right you are. I got the call from your paralegal and she said you had a breakthrough in our suit today. What happened?" A thrilled Piers waited expectantly for the good news.

Westmorland's faced screwed up into that intense, penetrating attorney's stare. "Come with me, Piers." He guided Piers into his office and offered him a seat, asking Casey to bring them something to drink.

"I'm sorry Piers, but there's no change in our suit. Who called you? What did they say, exactly?"

Piers sat back in his chair. It was like someone had punched all the air out of him. For a brief second he was angry but he bit his lip and answered, "Uh, she said she was your paralegal and you needed me to come for an appointment this afternoon."

"Give me a moment, Piers." Westmorland picked up his desk phone and called his paralegals.

Over the next five minutes, Westmorland spoke with each paralegal in his office. They all denied calling Piers. He thanked each in turn and hung up.

Both men considered the situation quietly and then Westmorland spoke.

"Piers, it occurs to me that someone wanted you out of your house today. I think you should call the police. Sounds like a burglary setup." He offered Piers the telephone on his desk. "Better have it checked out."

Acutely angry, Piers picked up the phone and dialed the Marsden-Lacey police station. Constable Cross answered.

"This is Piers Cousins and I think it may be necessary to have an officer go over to Healy and check things out. I received a call from someone pretending to be from my solicitor's office requesting that I come to Leeds. The appointment was bogus."

Constable Cross replied, "You're in Leeds? Odd. Chief Inspector Johns is waiting for you at The Grange, Sir. I'll call the Chief and he'll return your call. What is your number?"

Piers gave his mobile number to Constable Cross and hung up. He stood and made his way to the door.

"I've got to get back to Healy," he told Westmorland.

"Don't worry, Piers. You'll be hearing from me about the suit. I've finally got a tennis date next week with Judge Sutherland. He makes me play three brutal sets and then lets me buy him an expensive dinner. It's painful but effective." Westmorland shook Piers' hand in farewell.

Piers ran down the stairs and jumped into his Jaguar. Between Leeds and Marsden-Lacey, he chose to ignore every speed sign. He had one purpose: get back to Healy in time to stop a thief.

Chapter 36

Johns was at The Grange. Not a soul was about except a crow sitting in one of the mulberry bushes, cawing at him. His cell phone rang. It was the station. He hit "accept."

"Cousins is where? He thinks there's a burglary happening? Yeah, I understand, Cross. I'll call him." Johns ended the call and quickly dialed the number for Cousins' mobile phone. He motioned for Constable Waters to get out of her vehicle and come over to where he was parked.

Piers' voice came through the line. "Yes, this is Piers Cousins."

"Chief Inspector Johns. I've got a lot of questions to ask you, Mr. Cousins. I'll meet you at your home and I'm bringing another constable. What time can you be there?"

"Twenty minutes," Piers said and then he asked, "Chief, why were you waiting for me at The Grange today?"

"Your personal secretary phoned to tell me I couldn't have an appointment with you today because you had a meeting at The Grange. I wanted to stop by for a chat."

"Personal secretary? I don't have a secretary. Were you talking to someone at my house?"

Johns thought about the call and looked on his "recents" log in his phone. He read the number to Piers.

Johns could hear the strain in Piers' voice. "I don't recognize the number. A woman called me around noon to tell me my solicitor needed to see me in Leeds. I dropped everything… Oh Bloody Hell! Helen and Martha. They're at Healy. I completely forgot. They may be in danger. I forgot the girls were meeting there to go over my library."

Johns flipped a switch on his dash turning on the blue flashing emergency lights. He said he was on his way and hung up.

Leaning out through the window, he told Constable Waters to follow him and to not let Sam get out of the car once they arrived at Healy. With excellent car-handling skills, Johns accelerated until his vehicle was practically flowing like liquid metal through the narrow, rainy roads leading to Healy.

Scene Break

Martha couldn't see the entire kitchen from her vantage point. She turned to Helen. "If she's out there and sees me, let's turn around and run back down the passage. She might follow us but we could hide in these passages for days."

Helen was looking white-faced but she nodded her consent.

Only a few lights were on and the room was deathly quiet. Martha's only choice was to look around the corner. As she peeked, the hairs on the back of her neck stood up.

"Get up." A rough voice above her demanded.

A small circle of cold metal pressed against Martha's neck and an electric shock of fear seared through her body. She stood up, staring in the direction of the long kitchen work tables and gas ranges near the middle of the room.

The rifle barrel pushed her out into the room under an overhead light.

"Where's the other one?" the woman's voice demanded. "Come out, come out little mouse," she sang in a weirdly, childish sing-song tone. Then quickly shifted into, "or I'll kill your friend."

Helen stood up and moved out of her hiding place. She faced their assailant but wasn't able to recognize the woman standing in the shadows.

The tall kitchen windows were dark and streaked with rain. As a lightning bolt ripped across the sky, it illuminated the dimly

194

lit room in blinding flashes of light revealing for a few seconds the figure and face of Mrs. Thyme.

"You? But why?" Martha asked, completely baffled.

The normally tidy and professionally dressed housekeeper of Healy House was wearing a green waterproof hunting jacket opened at the neck, outdoor boots and thick gloves. Her grey hair was no longer in its usual tight bun. Pieces of her hair were still caught in hairpins at her nape, but most of it dangled in stringy wisps around her face and shoulders.

With her foot, Mrs. Thyme pressed an electric switch under the steel work table she was now standing behind. A row of utility lights came on illuminating the metal surface and casting a beam of light directly on the top of her head. She motioned for them to move over in front of the large walk-in freezers.

"That's better. I can see your pretty faces." She leveled the rifle at them again.

Martha could tell by Thyme's handling of the gun that she was comfortable with it in her hands. Her face was mostly in shadow due to the way the light hit only the top of the wide-brimmed felt hat she wore.

Mrs. Thyme said, "I don't have a problem with you, Mrs. Littleword, but Mrs. Ryes has to go. I've worked too hard to make a home for Emilia's child and I won't share it with another woman. Emilia's child needs a home and a mother, not another person to ship him off to a boarding school."

"I don't want to come between Piers and his child," Helen said.

Mrs. Thyme shook her head. "That's what they all say, but then they show their true colors. Most of them are like Lana Chason. She would have been bored with a child underfoot. I got rid of her though. Now, get in there." She motioned toward the walk-in freezer.

"I think I'd rather not," Martha said, trying to keep her talking. "You owe us an explanation other than you think Piers has a thing for Helen."

Mrs. Thyme laughed ruefully. "I don't owe you a thing." Then she lowered the gun barrel to right above Helen's head and fired.

The blast exploded above them and ricocheted around the kitchen, making Helen and Martha grab each other in terror. Nature, not wanting to be left out, discharged a stream of lightning across the nighttime sky, followed by a terrific boom of thunder.

SCENE BREAK

Piers, Johns and Donna followed each other down Healy's long drive. Martha's car sat forlornly in the drive. As everyone emerged from their vehicles, the storm broke above them. A streak of lightning crackled across the sky and simultaneously they heard what sounded like a rifle shot.

"Did you hear that?" Piers yelled at Johns over the rumble of thunder that immediately followed.

Johns heard the shot, and he knew the stakes had changed. "Waters! Come with me," he shouted over the storm. "Tell Sam *not* to get out of the car under penalty of death. You," he pointed at Piers, "stay here with the boy."

"Like hell I will. I'm coming with you." Piers bolted toward the front door.

Donna and Johns followed Piers into the hall where the fire was burning low. They were soaked from the lashing rain. Johns took his phone out of an inside coat pocket and called the station. He requested two constables come immediately to Healy.

"The shot came from the back of the house. What's back there?" he asked Piers.

"Mainly a conservatory and the kitchen."

"What is the fastest way to get to the back from the outside?"

"Outside entrance to the kitchen and conservatory. Go out here," Piers pointed to the main entrance, "and circumnavigate

196

around to your right. Can't miss it. One's glass and the kitchen has an old red-brick chimney attached to it."

Piers then turned to Donna. "We'll take the scenic route."

He motioned for her to follow him. They headed for a door under the massive oak stairwell in the Hall.

"Let's meet in the kitchen," Johns said as he headed out into the storm.

SCENE BREAK

Bored after five minutes alone in the police vehicle, Sam had run out of buttons to push. He rifled through Donna's purse but she only had ten pounds which he thought made her kind of pathetic. He didn't bother to swipe it.

Sam considered his entertainment options and then it hit him. What if he was an action hero? If he helped catch the thieves, he might get out of jail for performing an act of good citizenship. Probably get his picture in the paper. Penny would have to sit up and take notice.

Right about then a rare opportunity or maybe providence landed in Sam's lap. His phone rang. It was Penny. He nearly dropped the phone trying to accept the call

"Hi Sam. Saw your picture. You look so nice," Penny cooed.

Sam could hardly believe his ears. Donna was right. He decided to go for the goal. He lowered his voice and tried to imagine what Michael, the other constable at the station, would sound like talking to his girl if he were about to go into the line of fire.

"Hey Penny, can I call you back?" Sam asked in the lowest register of his voice. "I'm out working with the police on a burglary case. They've got some armed gunmen and I've got to help take these guys down."

Then to add effect, Sam yelled, "I'll be right there, Chief!"

To Penny, he said, "Got to go. I'll call you."

As he hung up the phone, he knew what he had to do. Sam got out of the car in the pouring rain and did his best Dirty Harry impersonation while walking up to Healy's front entrance.

SCENE BREAK

Helen and Martha huddled against the freezer's cold, steel surface after the lightening strike.

Mrs. Thyme said, "Get in there. No one will be coming home tonight. Piers is in Leeds and Agosto thinks he has a family crisis in Spain. Sarah got the night off to be with her boyfriend. So it's just us girls. I'll find you in the morning. It will be a terrible shock. We'll all be so sad. Get going!"

Martha opened the door and a blast of frosty air coiled around her. Utterly helpless, she walked inside with Helen behind her. They turned around to see the door shut with a terrible finality. The small freezer light stayed on for only a moment then they were in complete darkness.

"Tell me you have a pen light?" Martha asked.

"I don't." Helen's words were barely audible with the humming sound from the freezer droning above them.

The cold was insidious. It wrapped around them, making their flesh constrict. The darkness and the occasional cracking sounds from the crate Helen found to sit on was becoming intensely oppressive.

Martha, wearing only a T-shirt, started to shiver. She rubbed her hands up and down her arms while Helen felt the wound on her arm to see if it was still bleeding.

"I bet she's gone," Helen said through chattering teeth. "Do you remember the day we were here and Agosto shut himself in the other refrigerator? Thyme said then that he could get out because there was an emergency latch."

Martha swung around and felt for a latch. In the dark she couldn't find anything that might be a latch. Nothing. She threw herself against the door, pounding it with both fists, yelling, "I need a break today!"

To their horror, there was a click sound and the door slowly opened. As a crevice of light seeped into their dark, icy cave, they saw a young, handsome man with a goofy smile on his face.

"Hey, you want out of there?" he asked in an easygoing manner.

It took a second but then Sam and Martha recognized each other.

"You," Martha said, drawing out the word.

"You?" Sam answered, cringing.

Sam didn't have time to run because Martha grabbed the boy and gave him a huge, albeit cold, hug. She refused to let him go until Helen pried her arms free with statements like, "that's enough, Martha," and "the kid is probably scared."

Sam took it all with surprising grace.

"You're our hero, boy. We were going to freeze to death in there," Martha said joyfully with tears beginning to stream down her face.

"Well, you probably would have suffocated first," Sam said nonchalantly, which evoked horrified looks from both Helen and Martha. "Someone put a plastic cover over the ventilator. Might have kept you from getting oxygen."

This caused Helen to finally faint but not before Sam grabbed her. He put her down on the floor as Piers and Donna emerged from the same passage Helen and Martha used earlier.

Piers saw the three of them and rushed over to where Helen lay on the floor.

Donna grabbed Sam. "What on Earth are you doing here? Oh my God. The Chief is going to kill us both."

Martha grabbed Sam back from Donna and held on to his arm. "He saved our lives. We were locked in the freezer by that crazy housekeeper. Helen's been shot and we would have run out of air. This boy is my hero." Martha was rambling a bit and shaking from shock.

Donna looked stunned. Piers picked Helen up and carried her to a chair.

"She needs a doctor. Who did this Martha?" he asked.

"I just told you. Mrs. Thyme. She's a total nut job." Talking was helping Martha to feel less hysterical. "She's probably still here somewhere. She's got a gun. She tried to kill Lana."

Piers looked like he had been slapped and then punched. He sat down beside Helen and held her hand. Another piercing strike of lightning and the kitchen door slammed open. They all jumped and screamed as the Chief, wet as an otter, came in from the rainstorm.

"Chief," Donna said, "the woman who is at the heart of this is possibly still in the house and she's got a gun."

"No she isn't. She's locked in my backseat with cuffs on. She was trying to leave. What happened here?" He glanced at Helen's bloody arm and gave Sam a look of death.

Donna started to speak but Sam blurted out, "I think we should take these women somewhere more comfortable, Sir. They've had a terrible shock and one has been shot. Probably needs medical attention."

"I'm fine." Helen said, lucid again but still rather limp in her chair. "The bullet only grazed my arm. I think I'll live."

Johns looked at Constable Waters and smiled. He was angry with Sam but sometimes you had to be grateful for small mercies.

To Sam he said, "Fine idea. I'll need to see everyone at the station for statements. Sam, you ride with Waters. Mr. Cousins, would you please see Mrs. Littleword and Mrs. Ryes to the station? I'll have Doc Whithersby come by to check on them."

They all stared at Johns. No one was able to move.

"You have Mrs. Thyme in the police car already?" Martha asked, a bit dubious.

"Yes. She never saw me hiding behind the wall outside. Had a big shot gun with her. Grabbed her from behind. Tossed her into the car. Simple."

Something in Martha snapped. She went over to Johns and gave him a kiss on the cheek. "Thank you, Chief Inspector. Thank you for everything."

Johns looked down on Martha. Their eyes locked for a second.

"You're welcome, Mrs. Littleword."

SCENE BREAK

There was a slow progression of vehicles away from Healy. Helen and Martha sat in the back of Piers' Jaguar wrapped in blankets.

"Did she say why she wanted to kill you, Helen?" Piers asked softly while gripping the wheel with both hands.

"Yes. She also rambled something about Lana not being a good mother. Remember her saying that, Martha? I thought it odd at the time," Helen replied.

"She didn't want Helen moving in, Piers." It was a good sign that Martha's cheekiness was returning. She continued, "Thyme thought if the child came to Healy, she would get to mother him. Or maybe she had designs on you herself."

Piers was quiet for a few minutes. Then he said, "She was Emilia's nanny. I hired her ten years ago because she wanted to come back to England to be near Emilia. She was thrilled to know I might be getting custody of Emerson. I feel so terrible for putting you both in danger."

Helen was resting with her head nestled into the crook of Martha's shoulder. Martha was texting her daughter, Kate. She looked up and said, "It's okay, Piers. You didn't have anything to do with it. Probably ought to get that woman some serious psychological help, though." Then she went back to texting.

Piers shrugged. At least Martha was back to normal. He wondered what Mrs. Thyme would tell him once he got to the Marsden-Lacey Constabulary.

Chapter 37

Once everyone had given their statements, Johns put Mrs. Thyme into a secure cell and Constable Cross was given the serious task of keeping her safe and alive until the next morning.

Martha and Helen were checked out by Dr. Whithersby both medically and literally. An impressive bandage encircled Helen's arm and they were both given a sedative to take once they arrived home, something to let them relax so they would sleep deeply.

Penny put her engagement to the clod, Jeffrey Baldwin, on hold.

Piers drove the girls back to Flower Pot Cottage and again slept on the couch to give them a sense of safety.

Donna went home to her boys, two dogs and a husband who was trying to heat up leftovers with no success.

Johns drove home to his old farm house to find his mother testing two new beers she'd finished that afternoon. They deliberated deep into the night on the merits of both which in turn brought a very sound and peaceful sleep for the Chief.

SCENE BREAK

Bright and early the next morning, Perigrine and Alistair were busily pruning the bushes and weeding the beds around the constabulary when Donna arrived carrying her lunch.

"We have a tasty surprise for you, Donna Dear," Alistair said with a knowing grin. "Harriet heard all about Sam's heroism last night and sent over sticky buns, two sugar cakes and her famous shortbread for you."

"Wow! Am I supposed to eat all that?" Donna tried to juggle multiple bags.

"Here. Let me help you carry some of that." Helen came up behind her. "You've got more bags than arms."

"No. You're not supposed to eat it all yourself, Donna," an indignant Perigrine said. "You're supposed to share with your friends. Really. I don't know about you sometimes."

Alistair and Perigrine gave side looks to each other but Donna and Helen, with Martha in tow, ignored them and continued into the Constabulary.

Donna poked her head back out the door and called, "Are you two coming or what?"

Perigrine and Alistair put down their shears, checked each other for stray hairs and leaves, then gracefully ascended the stairs and went inside.

Johns came from out of the back area where the cells were housed.

"Is Cousins here?" he asked the girls.

"On his way. Had to park the Jag," Martha said with a smile.

Johns returned her smile. "The interview is going to take some time. Mrs. Ryes, would you please give us some of your expertise? The manuscript has been recovered and I would like your opinion once more about how we should proceed now that Mr. Devry is…well…dead."

"Of course, Chief Inspector. I would love to have more time to examine it and a colleague of mine at the Bodleian will be an excellent resource."

Perigrine and Alistair maintained delightfully inscrutable faces during this exchange but P. couldn't help himself. He gave Donna a pleading look and she intervened on his behalf.

"Chief, Perigrine has some affinity for works of art. Might he have a look?" she asked.

Johns shrugged and waved them all through. "Fine with me. Don't anybody get any ideas though. The evidence room is Marsden-Lacey's Tower of London. No one gets in or out without being frisked." He gave Constable Cross a stern look.

Perigrine could have kissed Donna for this treat of seeing the manuscript again and hearing Helen's assessment. He gave her a wink as he passed by on his way to the evidence room along with Helen, Martha, and Constable Cross. No chances were being taken with the manuscript this time.

The rest of the constables and Alistair sat down for morning coffee and gossip. Sticky buns were passed out and coffee was dispensed. So many stories needed to be straightened out and discussed in depth before misguided locals told misconstrued versions of the previous night's exciting events.

Chapter 38

Johns opened the door to Mrs. Thyme's cell. He motioned for Piers to wait a bit.

"Mrs. Thyme, I have Mr. Cousins to see you. Are you ready to have a visitor this morning?" Johns asked in a gentle manner.

He'd learned from so many years in the force that with patience and kindness, you can save yourself a great deal of time. They needed to start soon because the welfare worker sent up from Leeds to attend to Mrs. Thyme was waiting in the interview room. The department always had a welfare worker in the interview process, especially when they were dealing with a person so unstable.

Mrs. Thyme met his gaze but she appeared disoriented. Still curled up in a corner of her cot, she hugged herself and stared at Johns from the deep, scared eyes of an animal. But once Piers walked into the room, she uncoiled from her bodily knot and threw herself at him, clinging to his shoulders and weeping uncontrollably.

Piers patted her while shooting unsure glances at The Chief. Johns nodded and intimated he should keep up the assurances. After a few minutes she quieted down.

"Are you ready, Mrs. Thyme, to talk about what happened last night?" Johns asked in a calm and soothing tone.

Donna brought in a pot of tea and some of the wonderful treats Harriet had sent with Alistair.

Johns poured her a cup of tea which she picked up and cradled in her hands. After a short while she started. "I didn't want that woman to have Emilia's child. I didn't want any of them to have Emerson. Piers," she said pleadingly, "Emerson has had such a terrible childhood. Carstons was so brutal and he needed to die."

Johns and Piers looked at each other and then Johns spoke. "Did you feel you needed to kill Sir Carstons, Mrs. Thyme, to protect the child?"

She pulled herself upright in her chair. Her voice was indignant. "Well, someone had to do something. He killed his wife and he was going to ruin that child's life."

"What made you kill him so many years after Emilia's death?" Piers asked gently.

With swollen eyes filling with tears, she looked out through the window and appeared to be focusing on one of Perigrine's rose bushes. "Emilia called me over ten years ago and begged me to come to England to be close to her. You gave me the job. It nearly killed me to see how that brute of a husband emotionally tortured her. She had nothing, no money of her own to fall back on. The other worthless man in her life, her father, made her penniless to keep Carstons from getting his hands on her money. That's why her worthless husband abused her. He only saw money when he married her. Once he realized he would never get his hands on a penny of her fortune, he decided to mash her, torture her and crush her any way he could." Mrs. Thyme cried softly.

"I asked her to leave him, Hilda, but she wouldn't," Piers said in an apologetic tone. "She refused to see me after she found out about her pregnancy. I never knew what happened. Do you know why?"

Mrs. Thyme didn't speak for a bit. It was as if she was having trouble finding the right words. When she finally continued, she picked up and held Piers' hand, then said tenderly, "Emerson is not your child, Piers." She let the words lay there.

His gaze locked onto hers and he asked hoarsely, "Whose child is he?"

"Louis was his father," she answered in a dull tone.

They each looked for answers in the others' eyes but finding none, Piers finally asked. "Did you kill Louis, too?"

She took a deep breath and let it out. "Yes. He was a mess. Couldn't love anything. He had nothing but his own love for

Emilia. He was as addicted to his love of her as Carstons was to his need to torture her. Besides he didn't want Emerson. So weak, so pathetically weak."

"Hilda, why did you try to kill me?" Piers asked, confused.

"I didn't try and kill you. I wanted to kill that silly woman from Louisiana. You were dancing. It was hard to get a clean shot. She only wanted your money. Would have shipped Emerson off to some terrible school so she wouldn't have a messy child around the place. I nearly died when I saw you were the one I hit."

Piers looked down at Mrs. Thyme's hand still covering his own. Johns could see the tension Cousins was under.

"Why Helen and Martha, then?" Johns asked not wanting to lose the momentum of her confession.

Mrs. Thyme looked surprised to hear Johns speak, as if she'd forgotten he was in the room. "Oh, like I told them, I had nothing against Mrs. Littleword. I did push her down the stairs but after I talked with her later, I realized she didn't suspect me. It was Mrs. Ryes who was the real problem. She was just another woman who wouldn't want to deal with a small boy underfoot. In the end though, you couldn't kill one and not the other," she said almost flippantly then turned her attention back to Piers.

"Piers, you have to understand. Women see everything you are and everything you have. They can be so grasping and self-absorbed. It was only a matter of time before you brought home one to be your wife. It had fallen to me to get Emerson a safe home with you. I wasn't going to let Emilia's child suffer at the hands of one more selfish, evil person."

No one spoke for a few moments. Johns and Piers were trying to digest Mrs. Thyme's story and fathom her insanity at the same time.

"So you tried to shoot Lana, but you missed and got me?" he asked.

"I'm so sorry. I was so relieved you were okay, but there was a bright side. Miss Lana left that night and I haven't seen her since."

Johns and Piers gave each other quick, nervous looks and Johns scribbled a note on his legal pad: "Locate Lana Chason."

"Mrs. Thyme, how did you know Emerson was Louis' child?" Johns asked.

She looked at Piers.

"I read all of your mail, Piers. I know I shouldn't have. There was a letter from an attorney in Connecticut dealing with Emilia's estate and because you were the president of The Grange, they thought you might have an address for Louis. They'd written him at The Grange and he hadn't responded."

"Louis' sister said he shut down when he learned he was the father of Emilia's child," Johns said.

"Mrs. Thyme, did the attorney's tell you Louis was Emerson's father?" Piers asked.

"Yes, after I told them I was Louis' mother and he was dying."

Both Johns and Piers flinched at the irony of the comment. Johns shifted the questioning.

"Mrs. Thyme, will you please tell us how you killed Sir Carstons?"

"I always wanted him dead, but I saw him in the marketplace last Friday and I asked him about Emerson. I wanted to see the child," she said as her face darkened. "He told me to go to Hell."

Mrs. Thyme with her hands clasped in her lap, kneaded them together. "I followed him and saw him go into The Grange. There's a small alcove, you know, right inside the door. I picked up the rock holding the door open. It was shadowy and I could sit quietly and wait. I finally saw what I needed to do. He needed to die."

"Did you hear the conversation between Louis Devry and Sir Carstons?" Johns asked.

"Yes, and that was when I realized how I could get rid of two birds with one stone."

Johns and Piers kept still and waited for her to continue.

"I could hear feet coming quickly down the stairs, and Louis telling Sir Carstons he wasn't going to give him the manuscript. They argued and Carstons said he would see to it that Louis was turned over to the police for taking it from Harvard. Louis told him to get out and that he would turn it over to you, Piers, before he ever let Carstons get his filthy hands on it. I couldn't see Louis, but Carstons walked right past me. I thought I had missed my chance. I sat there for a little bit. Before I could come out from the alcove, a woman came breezing in through the doors. It was Mrs. Littleword."

"What happened to Carstons?" Piers asked.

"He must have been hiding while the woman was in the room because once she was gone, I didn't even have a chance to move before he walked right back through the doors. He was on the phone saying something about Mrs. Devry was ill. I picked the heavy rock up again and, while he was talking, I simply came up behind him."

"How did a piece of paper with my name on it get stuck to the rock?" Pierce asked.

Mrs. Thyme thought for a moment. "I don't know for sure. There was blood on my hand from the rock. I didn't have anything to wipe them clean but I found a tissue in my pocket. Maybe one of your cards I carry was stuck to the tissue and the rock when I tossed it over the hill."

Johns' got a tingly feeling. "Mrs. Thyme would you have seen the item they were struggling over?"

"I found it the next day under Louis' bed. I knew it was the same envelope as the one they'd been fighting over and that it must be valuable. But if Louis gave it to you, Piers, it wouldn't look like he needed to kill Sir Carstons. I wanted it to look like Louis had killed him. That way when he was found dead by suicide, the case would be closed. Then Louis was out of the picture, too."

Johns shifted the questioning. "Did you manipulate the surveillance videos?"

Mrs. Thyme looked bored by the question. "Piers' passwords were written in his address book. That was simple to manage."

"One last question, Mrs. Thyme. Helen and Martha found a piece of your glove in the garden. You must have known it was missing and yet you sent them out there anyway. Why?" Johns asked.

"I didn't realize about the glove. I saw later it was torn but I needed to get rid of them because they were snooping around too much. The dogs would attack anyone near that garden wall and they'd been trained to come up quietly on their target. Somehow those two escaped." She shrugged her shoulders.

"Did you follow them to The Grange, too?" Johns pushed a bit more.

"They told me they were going to The Grange that night. I knew where you kept your extra keys, Piers, so I thought I would make it look like a burglary and they'd gotten shot."

"They said the voice sounded strange. What were you using?"

She looked at Johns for a short moment then laughed and shook her head. "That was fun. The gardener's boy left a small machine you talk into and it makes your voice change. I did enjoy using that toy."

Then with a complete alteration in her demeanor, she put her hands together in a prayerful way and asked Piers, "Do you think you'll get Emerson, Piers?" Her eyes were tired and strained from the emotions she'd borne.

His first reaction was empathy so he went with that. "I hope so, Hilda."

"Will I be able to see him? Me a…murderer?" she asked simply.

Piers looked at Johns and Johns fielded the question.

"Mrs. Thyme, that's up to the court and the psychological evaluation."

She looked at Johns. "I don't regret one single thing I've done. Sometimes someone has to pay a price so that someone else can have what they need. All I want is for Emerson to be cared for and you'll do that for him, won't you, Piers?"

Piers nodded but his mind was reeling from the moral and emotional roller coaster he was experiencing. He reached across the table, took Mrs. Thyme's hand, and held it.

They all sat in silence for a minute. For the first time, Johns recognized and respected the character of the man holding Mrs. Thyme's hand. Then Donna opened the door to say the van from the hospital was there to take Mrs. Thyme and the social worker to the hospital in Wayford.

Scene Break

The group of admirers around the table in the evidence room were making lots of "ooh" and "ahh" sounds.

"So, what is it?" Johns asked, walking into the room with Piers.

Everyone around the table looked up immediately, each with an awed expression like they were beholding a miracle.

Helen, her voice raw with excitement, said, "In a million years you'll never believe what we have on this desk. Never. Never. Never."

Piers and Johns stood slightly dumbstruck in the doorway then quickly crossed the room to look at the manuscript laying on a clean, white, linen cloth.

Perigrine, with a tear in his eye and a voice raspy with emotion said, "It's Emily Brontë's missing novel. Priceless. Simply priceless."

"I've got goosebumps," Helen said.

Piers walked over and bent down. On a page stained from age, along a margin in a woman's delicate hand, was written a small poem. It was vaguely familiar to him. Here though, only a stanza of the entirety was written:

"Come walk with me, come walk with me;
We were not once so few
But Death has stolen our company
As sunshine steals the dew—
He took them one by one and we
Are left the only two."

The room was reverently quiet. Then Johns said, "Better call someone from Harvard. It's theirs."

The group looked up at him like he had stripped down to his shorts and was dancing the hoochie coochie.

"Why? What do you mean?" The room exploded with everyone talking at once, accusing Johns of various forms of unpatriotic, un-English, unfeeling coarseness.

"It's not ours! Devry stole it from Harvard!" Johns yelled, trying to get over the noise of all the people talking.

Everyone stopped mid-accusation.

"We have no choice," Johns said. "That's final. Lock it up, Cross, before it goes missing again."

He walked out of the room feeling relieved, completely above-board, and suddenly hungry. No time like the present for lunch he decided, so he found his way to the reception area and announced, "I'm going for lunch at The Traveller's, Constable Waters. Be back in an hour."

Donna made a mental note and went back to listening to Alistair tell her about the time they were saved from being arrested by the Polish police by a band of gypsies.

Things were back to normal in Marsden-Lacey. At least for a while.

Chapter 39

Marsden-Lacey, England
One Week Later

"So, I'll continue the inventory at Healy while you're gone. Think you'll have time to get a tan while you're in Florida?" Martha asked while helping Helen pack her suitcase for her trip.

Having retrieved a large majority of her things from her flat in Leeds, Helen was staying with Martha and sharing expenses while they worked on their extensive jobs in Marsden-Lacey. She was ready to give away her ex-husband and attend his wedding in Orlando. Leaving that afternoon, Helen was trying to find enough hot weather clothing to not die from the Florida heat.

"So, did you invite Piers to go or did he invite himself?" Martha pumped Helen for information.

"I absolutely did not invite him. He brought it up because he has friends in Key West. I told him if he would like to have dinner one night while we are both there, we could meet. I'm still a bit stung by how people might perceive my intentions about him."

"Oh for Pete's sake, Helen. Thyme was a nut job. She doesn't count. I think you should have some fun and show him off to your ex and his floozy."

"Why don't you worry about your own love life?" Helen threw a pair of frilly knickers back at Martha who'd tried to stuff them into Helen's case.

The doorbell rang as Martha threw the undies back at Helen but they landed on Amos' head instead.

"You might want those. You'll wish you'd packed them," Martha called over her shoulder before running down to answer the front door.

She found Chief Inspector Johns blocking the sun on her doorstep.

"Why hello, Chief Inspector. What can I do for you?"

"I wondered if you would like to go to dinner tonight, Mrs. Littleword?" he asked.

She blinked up at him. The sun had turned him into a dark silhouette filling her door.

"Please come in," she said, a bit rattled. This was the last thing she'd expected. "I can't this evening. I have a date tonight, but maybe another night?" She gave him a big, bright smile.

Johns stayed his usual rigid self. "Oh, I see. Wouldn't be with anyone I'd know?"

"Well, maybe. Do you remember the doctor you had come to the station after everything happened at Healy? You had him check us over. Gave Helen a mammoth bandage for her arm?"

"Whithersby." Johns growled lowly as his face grew dark.

"Yes. That's him. Well, he's been such a nice man, coming here almost every day to check on me. He's concerned I might have pulled something in my back while trying to flee from Mrs. Thyme," Martha said, getting wrapped up in her own vision of herself as a gothic heroine.

"Fine," Johns said tersely. "I hope you have a wonderful time, Mrs. Littleword. I wouldn't be too sure of the Doc, though. He sometimes tips the bottle a wee bit more than he should."

Martha's eyebrows knitted as if concerned by what he said.

Johns nodded. "And he can be something of a rake."

"A rake, you say?" She grinned as Johns glowered.

"It's a concern. For a lady, like yourself."

Martha found it difficult not to laugh. "I appreciate your warning, Chief. I'll do my best not to let Dr. Whithersby threaten my reputation."

Johns grunted, stood straighter. "Good. I'll look forward to another time then...perhaps."

He gave her a strained smile and turned down the pathway leading to her gate.

Martha stood in the doorstep, one hand on her rounded hip while a new addition to the family menagerie, a tabby, Maine coon cat, threaded lovingly between her ankles. With a knowing smile on her lips, Martha considered Johns' back side.

"Not bad. Not bad at all," she thought, then quietly shut the door and ran back upstairs to help Helen pack for her Floridian fun.

Made in the USA
Monee, IL
16 July 2020